The Titanium Mysteries Book 12:

The Bank

Ali Noel Vyain

This is a work of fiction. Names, characters, places, and incidents either are the product of the author's imagination or are used fictitiously. Any resemblance to actual persons, living or dead, events, or locales is entirely coincidental.

Copyright © 2024 by Ali Noel Vyain.

No part of this book can be reproduced or used in any manner without written permission of the copyright owner.

Elsewhere

1st edition printing

alinoelvyain.wordpress.com

Contents

Chapter 1 Rebuilding 1
Chapter 2 Nebula Reprised 10
Chapter 3 Xenocryst is Called 20
Chapter 4 The Former Police Captain . . . 30
Chapter 5 Nightmare 41
Chapter 6 Another Body 51
Chapter 7 Decoys 60
Chapter 8 Connections 70
Chapter 9 The Special Bank 79
Chapter 10 Shamanic Journey 89
Chapter 11 Plan 100
Chapter 12 Magic 108
Chapter 13 Werewolf Wedding 118
Also By Ali Noel Vyain 128

Chapter 1 Rebuilding

The people of Tigerwood were just beginning to recover from the bombs. Those who had survived were easing back into their normal lives. Some were just coming out of the hospital. Others were more relaxed and no longer worried about bombs going off in their city. And there was rebuilding going on in the most of the destroyed areas.

Charm School wasn't being rebuilt. Instead, the debris was cleaned up and the rest of the building was removed. At the shopping center, debris was removed and stores were being rebuilt. At the open air cafe, the debris was removed and the cafe was in the process of being rebuilt.

As for the site of the first bank, the debris had been removed and another bank had been built. This new bank claimed to be a special bank which helped those in need. Willow, as many others in Tigerwood, had heard of the new bank. She walked around the area on her way from market.

She blinked when she saw it. She walked around it and discovered it was hard to breathe. Then it hit her. There was something wrong with the bank itself. She stopped walking and stared at the building.

It seemed so ordinary and not much different from the first bank that was in this same spot. Willow frowned. Something was wrong and she could feel it. She wasn't sure about going inside of it. That would only increase the feeling of dread and hopelessness. She blinked and focused on her breathing.

She was well aware that most people wouldn't be able to feel what she was feeling from the bank. She resumed walking around it. She continued to take deep breaths as she concentrated on the bank itself. She walked closer to the building where there weren't any pedestrians. She raised her right hand and touched it.

Instantly, she felt herself transported into the dark. She heard people screaming in agony. She blinked, but there wasn't much to see. Only to feel and think.

"What is this place?" she asked.

Someone gasped. "Get out of here! It's not safe for you to be here with us! We're all trapped!"

She felt someone push her backwards. She fell to the sidewalk and blinked in the sunshine. She focused on her breathing as she gaped at the bank. She blinked and knew there were trapped souls inside. Souls who had just warned her and protected her.

She thought to the trapped souls without moving her mouth. "Thank you for saving me. I want to set you all free. Do you know how I can do that?"

Another soul answered her in her head. "We made contracts and this is our punishment for breaking them."

Willow continued to gape. She picked herself up and grabbed

her things. She walked home as quickly as she could. It wasn't until she was inside and putting away her things that she heard someone else enter the house. She gasped and turned around to see Waldo. She sighed in relief.

He blinked. "Why are spooked? I've never seen you like this even though I look just like my dead brother."

She took a deep breath. "I went shopping for supplies today and walked past the new bank. It felt awful to be near it. I felt the building and discovered some trapped souls who pushed me away to save me. They think they are being justly punished."

He raised an eyebrow. "That's creepy. I think you need to cleanse yourself of that bad energy."

"Yes, I should do that. I want to help those trapped souls. They were screaming in agony. No punishment is worth that."

"What are they being punished for?"

"They said they broke their contracts."

"Hmm." He grabbed the sage and lit it. "Here, just let it go for now. I'm sure when the time is right, you'll figure out what you need to do to free those trapped souls."

He waved the sage around her body. She breathed in the sage and relaxed. He cleansed himself too. Then he cleansed the things she just brought home and the whole house. She smiled as she watched him cleansing everything.

She wondered how she got so lucky with this one. They were still together without any trouble. Unlike her many other lovers, this one was interested in magic and had some natural talent. He also focused on harmless and healing magic. She wondered if having an identical twin had anything to do with it.

When he was done, he snuffed out the sage and left in on the altar. She walked over to him and put her arms around his neck. He put his arms around her waist and held on to her. He was glad he had found her even though his own twin was her former lover.

Time lost all meaning to the couple as they held on to each other. For now they needed to rest and tend to their daily lives. Later they would do something for the trapped souls.

Zanthe took a deep breath. She had registered at a local university and Zelda had given the werewolf a good reference. Now, Zanthe was waiting for her test results. Zane was taking a shower. Her tablet beeped and she checked it. She blinked and then cheered.

Zane came out of the bathroom moments later. "What are you so happy about? Is it about the test results?"

She nodded. "Yes, I passed with flying colors. So, I have some class credits."

He smiled. "That's great. When do you start classes?"

"Oh, next week. However, they are online, so that shouldn't be a problem with my work."

"Even better. I bet they will give you homework with deadlines."

"Shouldn't be a problem. I can do it on my tablet computer without any trouble."

"So, what should we do now? Should we look into getting wedding clothes? Or try and find Cipher's last hideout?"

"Hmmm. I think we should go get wedding clothes and then we can go look for the hideout. Will Nebula being willing to help us with whatever we find?"

"They might. I'll send them a message and see what they say."

"Okay, sounds good."

They left the home they shared to go shopping. They walked together. So much happiness without any worries about any new cases to deal with. They spent time finding the right clothes which fit them well and went together as a couple. They didn't go for anything traditional as it didn't matter to either one of them.

Jaema and Zelda were cuddling together as were Zeta and Julian. They were watching another episode of Alara and Oliver.

Jaema asked, "How does everyone feel about Zanthe and Zane getting married?"

Everyone smiled.

Zeta answered, "I'm happy for them. I know he was confused when they first met, but now knows it's okay."

Julian nodded. "He actually came to me for advice. I was shocked. I just told him what Zelda and I did when it happened to me. It worked out for us."

Zeta smiled. "I'm so glad it did. I didn't expect you."

Julian asked, "So, you're still happy with me?"

Zeta answered, "Yes."

Zelda smiled. "I do think they make a good couple. They both deserve to be happy after all they've been through. It's just interesting it didn't happen until they were older. Seems to me, people expect it to happen when we're young."

Zeta said, "That's just a myth. For some people it happens when they're young, but not for everyone. Or they don't get it right the first time."

Julian said, "Either way, we have a wedding to attend soon."

Zelda said, "A new case could interrupt their wedding."

Zeta blinked. "Did Zanthe apply for school?"

Zelda nodded. "She did. I know she was accepted and had to take some tests to assess where she's at. I do hope they give her some credit for the work she's already done. That should save her some time."

Jaema asked, "Does it bother you that she was able to get the job without a degree?"

Zelda blinked. "I don't know. I did find it a bit odd at first, but she's proven herself. She's got a good head on her shoulders. I'm sure with the pack patrolling the woods helped her too.

The wolves have been quite helpful lately."

Zeta smiled. "They do take that job seriously. I know they aren't afraid of the police now and know when to tell them or just tell the werewolves when something bad happens. Such as when someone is in the woods at night that shouldn't be there."

Zelda smiled. "There is that. The police have told me how helpful the wolves are. Sometimes people get lost and don't get out of the woods before night falls. So, the wolves help the people get out safely."

Julian said, "That's a good thing. I'm glad the wolves can help out."

Jaema said, "I've been reading some posts on social media in regards to the wolves. People say they're surprised when they find themselves in the woods at night. Then some wolves show up and escort out them out safely."

Zeta added, "I've seen those too. I just let them know that's what the wolves choose to do. We've had too much trouble with people causing problems in the woods. The wolves are protecting their home and know when we're not supposed to be there. They tend to know what our intentions are and just help the lost ones get out safely. Otherwise they will report malicious intent to the werewolves or even the police."

Julian said, "I just feel safer knowing the wolves are helping to keep Tigerwood safe. I don't know what we'd do without them."

Zelda chuckled. "We'd be doing the same thing we are now."

Julian chuckled. "I know that. I meant I don't know how we did without their help in the past."

Jaema's tablet chimed. "Oh, that's a text message for Xenocryst." She checked it. "Uh, we might have a new case. Willow isn't sure about the new bank."

Julian asked, "You mean the one that replaced the first one?"

Jaema answered, "That's the one."

Zelda said, "A bank was mentioned to Nebula by Cipher. So, what did Willow notice?"

Jaema blinked. "This is interesting and sounds quite creepy." She took a deep breath. "She thinks the bank has some trapped souls in it that are being tortured. She's not sure what she could do to free them just yet, but the souls mentioned to her about breaking contracts."

Zeta sighed. "That's not good. Who would want to trap souls when people break their contracts?"

Zelda blinked. "I'm sure we'll have to find out. Cipher is dead and the former police captain is in prison. Nebula doesn't know much about it. So, who's still alive that would know?"

Julian said, "We'll have to talk to the werewolves about what all the former police captain did before he was arrested."

Jaema blinked. "I see some people are giving the new bank some good reviews."

Zeta asked, "Any bad reviews?"

Jaema shook her head. "I don't see any. That can't be a good sign. Usually, when there are good reviews without any bad ones, it means the business has given people incentives to give good reviews."

Zeta said, "Right and that could mean the business is hiding something. No one has a perfect business rating. It's impossible to please everyone. I would think someone would be unhappy with the bank. That's just normal."

Zelda blinked. "I can see that. So, what is this bank hiding?"

Zeta answered, "I wonder if they use souls as collateral for loans?"

Julian said, "That's too simple. I don't get it. Are we missing something?"

Zeta shrugged. "We figured out who the terrorist was last time and discovered there was someone behind them. Perhaps this case will turn out that way."

Zelda said, "We'll see. Using souls for collateral is strange and I doubt many will accept it as a real case."

Zeta said, "We've solved cases involving vampires, werewolves, zombies, androids, penguins and an unusual shapeshifter. I'm sure souls are just the next logical step in what we have to deal with."

Julian said, "Perhaps you're right."

Chapter 2 Nebula Reprised

Nebula,

Zanthe and I have discovered the last hideout you shared with your father. We have some questions as to what we found left behind. Would you be willing to meet us here to enlighten us?

Zane

Zane,

I'd be happy to tell you what I know. I am grateful for all the help you have given me. You gave me a way out and I've been learning so much now. I have more friends too. So, what you ask isn't something I want to turn down. It's the least I can do after my just punishments for the things I've done.

Nebula

Zane showed Zanthe the messages. They looked at each other and then left the home they shared to go to the hideout the police had found. It took them some time to walk through the woods and find the hideout, but once there, they were able to get inside without any trouble.

   They planned to search room by room examining whatever they found. A mist floated near them and then formed into a human that fluctuated form constantly.

Zanthe said, "Hello, Nebula."

Nebula smiled. "Hello, Zanthe and Zane. This room was Father's."

Zane said, "I see." He held up a tablet computer. "Was this his?"

Nebula nodded. "I think he encoded his information to hide it."

Zanthe asked, "Do you know how to access the information on it?"

Nebula shrugged. "I'm not sure. Father never let me use his tablet. But he did teach me a lot of things Mother never could."

Zane said, "Perhaps from what you know about your father can help us unlock the information stored on this device."

Nebula blinked. "I can see that's possible. It's like when I suspected he killed Mother. Not just from the evidence of the animal attacks, but from what he said to me."

Zane nodded. "Alright. In that case, we give you the tablet to take back to the Guardian Hold so you can unlock it."

Nebula accepted the tablet. The werewolves went into another room. It was the medical area. Zane checked the computer and quickly found information on different treatments Cipher had received and one from Nebula after he had been shot by Zelda.

Zane looked at Nebula. "We heard Zelda shot you and here is the documentation of the care you needed as a result."

Nebula looked at the screen. "I remember that. She had every right to shoot me. Father wanted me to seduce both Zeta and Jaema. I chose Zeta first and she knew I wasn't her husband."

Zanthe smiled. "She told us your eyes were wrong."

Nebula nodded. "I believe she said the same thing to me. I was under Father's orders at the time, but when she reacted the way she did, I knew it was wrong and so I accepted the shot as a just punishment. I never complained about it and just took it."

Zane asked, "Didn't it hurt?"

Nebula nodded. "It did. I was willing to feel that pain. I needed to know what it felt like especially after the damage and pain I caused with the bombs."

Zane nodded. "Well, according to this information, the damage to you wasn't that bad. You just had to clean the wound and let it air out. I bet it's your shapeshifting abilities which saved you from any permanent damage."

"That's what the doctors tell me. They said that last bomb should have killed me as it did Father."

Zanthe said, "We remember watching it. You changing your shape when you did saved you."

Nebula said, "The doctors also thought the other bombs were causing some damage to my body, but it wasn't that noticeable at first. I know it became more apparent when I was alone with Ariana, but it never bothered her."

Zanthe smiled. "I think she likes it to some extent. She told me before she decided to become a sex worker that she didn't care which boy she was doing it with."

Nebula smiled. "Sometimes she asks me to look like someone else when we do it."

Zane smiled. "Alright, let's check out another room."

The bathroom was a quick check and then it was onto the kitchen. The werewolves checked the supplies that were quite scant at this time.

Nebula blinked. "I have since learned that Father didn't know much about what healthy food is."

Zanthe raised an eyebrow. "So, highly processed things. I don't see how anyone can cook in this kitchen."

Nebula said, "I wasn't taught how to cook and I doubt Father knew how. Ariana and I are trying to learn, but as you can see from my fluctuating form, I can't get to in person classes. I have to learn via screen. I don't like to upset people with my form. I know it can be disturbing to see me like this."

Zane smiled. "It certainly can be. However, Zanthe and I are used to shapeshifting ourselves that we know what you're doing even if you're not in full control of it."

Nebula smiled. "The other shapeshifters where I live can handle it too. Sometimes they give me tips on how to cook."

Zane looked around. "Is there just one more room in this hideout?"

Nebula nodded. "It was my room."

They walked into the last room. Nebula waited for questions.

Zanthe said, "I don't see much else here. Just a few pieces that you probably used when making bombs."

Nebula nodded. "There were always some leftover pieces. Father didn't know what all I would need, so he just give me lots of random pieces to use."

Zane said, "Other than clothes and other daily living things, there's nothing else here that we can see." He pulled out his tablet computer and scanned the area. "Looks like we found everything."

Nebula blinked. "I need to get back home now. I'll let you know what we find out from Father's tablet."

Zanthe said, "Thanks for your help, Nebula."

Nebula bowed and then transformed into a mist which floated out of the hideaway and disappeared.

Zane smiled. "Well, this has been interesting."

"How so?"

"Nebula is more cooperative than I would expect. I do hope they can unlock Cipher's tablet."

Zanthe nodded. "If anyone can, I would think they would be able to. Nebula knows Cipher better than anyone else currently living."

"I think you're right about that." He paused to put his tablet away. "I want to check the data from the medical computer again."

They walked back to the medical bay. He checked the data.

"Hmm. That's what I thought. The computer has documentation on Cipher as a were with several different forms."

Zanthe raised an eyebrow. "I see there are pictures too."

Zane asked, "I wonder why he would let this computer record all that information on him. I don't understand why he didn't hide how many forms he has. I would have thought he'd know medical computers aren't always secure."

Zanthe smiled. "Perhaps he didn't know that Guardians have a way of accessing medical computers without any trouble."

Zane smiled back. "Perhaps not. Or else he left it unsecured so Nebula could use the computer too."

"There is that. Are medical computers ever secured?"

"I don't think domestic models are typically, but I get the impression from Cipher that he was paranoid about security. Leaving this computer unsecured isn't a good idea with information on his different animal forms."

"Hmm. Is there a way to secure medical computers so only certain people can use them?"

"Yes, of course there is. Hospitals do it all the time to keep patients' information safe and secure."

"I see. Then what are we missing?"

Zane pulled out his tablet computer and scanned the medical computer. "Hmm. Oh, now I see what happened."

Zanthe looked at his tablet. "Cipher did secure the computer and Nebula unsecured it." She chuckled. "That appears to be an act of rebellion on Nebula's part."

Zane nodded. "I think so too. Cipher didn't think Nebula would need the medical computer and it was secured just for him and not his child. That's definitely not love."

"So, Nebula needed to unlock the computer to receive medical care. Which would mean, it's not entirely rebellion."

"I think it's safe to hope Nebula can unlock Cipher's tablet."

She smiled. "I'm so glad Nebula is working with the Guardians now. Nebula's money has made a huge difference in the rebuilding."

"I noticed that too. I haven't heard complaints about medical care expenses either."

"No, all their money covered it all. It's actually a relief when we can't keep Nebula locked up anywhere."

"They are maturing and are much better than they were when we met them."

"Ariana says the same thing too."

"Hasn't she grown up since we first met her too?"

She nodded. "Yes, she has. She has found someone she can commit to and who's committed to her in return."

He smiled. "I'm happy for them. I just hope we can get married soon, but unfortunately, there probably will be a case in the way."

"I get that feeling too. We can get married once we completely solve it."

"It's always good when one partner understands the other's work."

She laughed. "We're working together. I just wonder how we will be able to do our work with a baby."

"That might be difficult, but perhaps we can take time off and just focus on the baby."

"Wait, are you saying you want one with me?"

He smiled. "Perhaps. As you would be the one carrying the baby, I'll leave it up to you."

"Very well."

He put his tablet away and kiss her on her check. She kissed him back. Then they left the hideaway. They said nothing on their walk back through the woods. Instead they relaxed and accepted their relationship was going well and that another case might present itself all too soon.

Their walk through the woods was pleasant. The animals living there were used to the werewolves and didn't stop their daily activities. The animals knew they were safe from the werewolves. Zane and Zanthe just focused on their walk.

The pack greeted the werewolves and they greeted back. The pack didn't have anything to report other than the usual activities of day campers and hikers. No one was disrespecting the animals or the woods.

There was news of more births in the woods. The happy parents had their paws full. Others in the woods made sure they had plenty of food and were safe from any visitors.

Zane said, "It's good to hear the animals look after each other here."

Zanthe said, "I think they feel safer knowing there are plenty of us who care about them and their home."

"I'm sure it helps."

The werewolves saw a few hikers in other parts of the woods. The wolves kept patrols on the hikers to ensure everyone in the woods would be safe. It wasn't just the wolves anymore. Other animals kept watch and the visitors didn't know that's what the animals were doing. The hikers were too busy following the path through the woods to pay much attention to the animals.

The werewolves finished their walk and left the woods. They found their home where they had left it. They got inside and began writing up notes on what they had discovered at the hideout.

It wasn't much yet, and they were curious as to what information Cipher hid on his tablet computer. By that time, Nebula was back in their home where they set the Cipher's tablet out on a table. They stared at it and wondered if this was going to be like the time they had unlocked the medical computer.

Nebula blinked and Ariana came inside. She smiled at them. "I see you're home."

They looked up at her. "Yes." They paused. "I saw the old hideout with Zane and Zanthe. I tried to help them understand what we did there."

"Oh? How did it go?"

"Zanthe thanked me for my help. Zane gave me Father's tablet to see if I can unlock it."

"Oh, I see." She sat down across from them. "So, you are still helping."

"I think I should. I know Tigerwood has been rebuilding and things are better after the bombs. I guess they are hoping for some more information on the special bank which is there now."

Ariana sighed. "Can you unlock the tablet?"

Nebula shrugged. "I'm about to find out. I did unlock the medical computer and I was able to because of what I knew about Father."

"So, this tablet could be the same thing."

"This is worse in some ways. I know there will be more information on Father's illegal and wrong activities."

Ariana took their hand.

Chapter 3 Xenocryst is Called

Zane and Zanthe were enjoying dinner when the pack howled. The werewolves dropped their utensils and stepped off the ship. They walked quickly to the woods to see the wolves.

"Zane, it's a body."

"Just when I thought we had time to study up on what the former police captain did and finish planning our wedding, we get another case."

She sighed. "I suppose it was going to happen sooner or later." She used her watch to call the police.

They came within minutes and searched for clues with the werewolves. Other than the body, not much else was found. Zanthe wasted no time in calling Xenocryst Agency to help with the possible murder.

"Zane, does anything look off to you about the body?"

"No visible signs of a struggle. Or even of what the cause of death could be."

She nodded. "So, natural causes?"

Zane raised an eyebrow. "Not likely if they are in the woods."

"That's what the pack is saying. They aren't sure it was natural causes."

"What else does the pack think?"

"They are insisting someone dumped the body here to hide it."

The police took the body away without complaint. The werewolves continued to look for clues.

"Zanthe, this is weird. I think the pack is right. It appears on the ground that the body was dumped here and probably already dead."

"I'm sure the coroner will let us know as soon as they know something."

"As always."

"I wonder if there's any connection between the former police captain, Cipher and the new bank."

He studied her face a moment. "That's certainly a possibility. I don't see how they are, but we'll get to the former police captain's documents."

She nodded. The pack barked a greeting to Detectives Zelda and Julian. The werewolves looked in the direction of the barking.

Zane smiled. "Welcome, detectives. The body has just been removed."

Julian said, "No matter. Any clues so far?"

Zanthe answered, "The pack said the body was dumped here and Zane noticed the indentations on the ground which support that."

The detectives looked where the body was.

Zelda said, "I can see that. Any marks on the body to give us a clue as to how they died?"

Zane shook his head. "Nothing whatsoever. We're waiting on the coroner to enlighten us."

Julian said, "Of course. I find it odd there's nothing else here."

Zelda frowned. "So am I. Other than what the pack told you and what we see. Yeah, it's odd."

Zane said, "This is interrupting our wedding plans."

The detectives smiled.

Zanthe said, "Perhaps we'll hear from Nebula soon."

Zane said, "I hope so."

Zelda said, "We heard about the new bank opening where the first one was."

Julian said, "Not sure what the appeal is of that bank. Was it the one Cipher referred to?"

Zanthe answered, "We think it is. There are some references in the correspondences the former police captain left behind. Zane and I were about to go through that tomorrow when the pack notified us of the body."

Zelda said, "You can still do that tomorrow. That might be relevant to this case if not the prior ones."

Zanthe blinked. "How about you two come to the station tomorrow and we can see which cases you already solved and if there's a connection to the current one."

Zelda nodded. "I think that's a great idea. How are your classes so far?"

Zanthe smiled. "Not bad. I was able to test out of the easier ones. So, I'm getting into the things I missed."

Zelda smiled. "So, you're finding the classes interesting."

Zanthe nodded. "I think your reference helped. I do have to take some tests, but I do fairly well on them."

Zelda nodded. "Good. I'm willing to help you if you find you have too many questions."

Zanthe said, "Thanks. I was hoping I could ask you."

Zane said, "I left my tablet on our ship."

Julian said, "I think we've seen enough here. How far away is your ship?"

Zane answered, "Not far. We need to go this way."

Everyone followed Zane back to the ship. He quickly found his tablet computer and checked for messages. There was one from Nebula. He read it.

He blinked and looked up at everyone. "Nebula unlocked Cipher's tablet. They're sending me all the data on it."

Zelda blinked. "That's a lucky break."

Zane nodded. "Nebula unlocked a medical computer Cipher had secured and so I'm not entirely surprised. Oh, this is a lot of data." He kept reading. "Isn't Xavier, Zeta's uncle?"

Julian answered, "Yes. We caught him doing illegal activity."

Zane said, "Cipher had dealings with him and the former police captain. This goes back years."

Zelda looked at the information. "Oh, now I see it. No wonder the police captain didn't like us. It was worse after we called for help from the Guardians."

Zane said, "It's overwhelming. There's a lot here. I think we need to cross reference this with the former police captain's documents."

Zanthe said, "I see some references to the special bank. They've been planning it for years, but couldn't find a location in Tigerwood for it."

Julian said, "I see that. Amazing they kept at it for so long. It is hard to fight against determination."

Zane said, "You're both quite determined too and Cipher wasn't happy about that."

Zanthe chuckled. "Well, I'm glad the detectives are determined. Tigerwood needs your help."

Zelda said, "We're happy to answer the call."

Julian said, "It's what we do best." He paused to continue reading. "Looks like most of this are cases we've already solved."

Zanthe said, "That's somewhat comforting. But we're not sure about this current one."

Zelda said, "We just don't have enough information yet. We just have one dead body."

Zane said, "We'll find more clues. Clearly, there are plenty from Cipher and the former police captain. He is not getting out of prison anytime soon."

Zanthe said, "Not with all the information we have from him now. I think we can keep him behind bars. I don't see how we can let him out again with all this coming to light now."

Julian said, "He really was working against us for a long time."

Zelda said, "No wonder our shared office was in the basement. He was trying to isolate us. He never intended for us to solve those cases."

Zane said, "Yet, you did. How aware were you of his treatment of you?"

Zelda shrugged. "I knew he was prejudiced and I thought I just had to prove myself."

Julian said, "I wasn't paying attention that closely. I had a good partner to work with and didn't care until we were fired."

Zelda nodded. "I remember you got a tent and camped out in Zeta's yard."

Julian smiled. "I had to go somewhere and I didn't have permission to sleep in her house."

Zelda said, "And you didn't ask if you could sleep on the couch in mine."

Julian said, "Guilty as charged."

Zanthe said, "At least you two had a place to go. That always helps in times of crisis."

Zane said, "Like that time when you went to stay at Charm School?"

Zanthe nodded. "That was surprising to me, but I'm glad Ms. Clayborne let me stay there."

Zelda smiled. "How ironic that you were kicked out of the school and then allowed to go back after the teachers were murdered."

Zanthe smiled. "It certainly was ironic. I do think we have some clues here with information from both the former police captain and from Cipher that can help with this current case. I just don't see the connection yet."

Zelda said, "I think you're right there is one. At least we can keep ourselves busy while we wait on whatever the coroner can find out."

Zanthe's tablet beeped. She checked it. "Oh, it's from the coroner. They say they can't find a cause of death. The person was in good health and it definitely wasn't natural causes."

Zelda frowned. "This doesn't sound right."

Zanthe showed everyone the information.

Zelda sighed. "So, it's true. No apparent cause of death. So, we're not sure it was even murder. Yet, they didn't die of natural causes."

Zane blinked. "I wonder what Eugenia can tell us from the ghost."

Julian said, "I hope she can learn something. I'm starting to get a bad feeling about this case."

Zelda said, "Like this is the hardest one we've had to deal

with. Not many clues and yet someone is dead. I don't like it."

Zane said, "I don't like it either. No signs of magic either. That's not helping us."

Zanthe sighed. "I guess this case is just going to be hard for us no matter what."

Zane said, "We'll get through as we have the rest. We can't give up yet."

Zanthe smiled. "Even though we don't have many clues."

Zelda said, "We have lots of data to cross reference. I think we need Zeta to help with the data."

Zanthe said, "She's welcome to come tomorrow too. I'm sure she'd know better than the rest of us as she writes books about each case after you complete them."

Julian said, "We'd be lost without Zeta. I know she stays in the background, but she does so much."

Zelda smiled. "Jul, you just pay more attention to her than anyone else does. We'll tell her about the meeting when we get home."

Julian asked, "Do you need us anymore now? I would like to see my wife tonight."

Zane smiled. "In that case, go home and see your wife. Zanthe and I should take a break and work on our wedding."

Julian smiled. "Good. We are planning on coming."

Zelda smiled. "Jaema and I are planning on coming too."

Zanthe smiled. "Good. I invited Ariana and Nebula, but I

don't know if they can make it."

Zane said, "We'll find out soon enough."

The detectives left and walked home. The werewolves started in on wedding planning. They had their outfits and now they decided to work on their vows. Zane found Willow willing to perform the ceremony.

"Zanthe, is all this planning making you nervous?"

She bit her lip. "Perhaps a little."

"I know I'm getting nervous."

"I'm worried about school, the current case and the wedding. I do hope I can complete school, solve the case and marry you."

"We are working on all of that."

She sighed. "Did you ever think you would find someone you'd want to spend the rest of your life with?"

"No. I was beginning to wonder if there was anyone for me."

"I was thinking that. I just accepted I would be alone. I didn't even try to look for anyone."

"I was busy doing my Guardian work. I never worried about it. I know my parents were wondering, but they never gave me a hard time for it."

"That's good. My mother was disappointed I never got married. It hasn't bothered me until now. I know we need to finish planning and I want to get my degree first. Now we have a mysterious case. I just hope our wedding isn't delayed too long."

He chuckled. "I hope our wedding isn't delayed either. I'm

ready to fully commit to you. Then we can worry about whether we want to have children."

She smiled. "I'm glad you listen, even if you don't fully understand."

"Have you told your mother?"

"No. Do you want me to?"

"I think it would be a good idea. I'm sure she'd go into shock."

It was her turn to chuckled. "I'm sure she would too. I think she was beginning to think I don't like men. Alright, I'm sending her a message about it now."

She blinked and looked at him when she was done. He kissed her cheek. Her tablet beeped and she checked it.

"Zane, she is shocked. She wants to meet you."

"We've already met."

They laughed and kissed. Then they set up a time to meet with her mother so she could see him again.

Chapter 4 The Former Police Captain

In their shared office, the werewolves went over the correspondences and virtual paperwork left behind from the former police captain. There was a lot of material to go through, but they didn't mind as they figured it could help the current case.

They also now had the data from Cipher's tablet. They were busy cross referencing the information between the two sources when Julian, Zelda and Zeta entered their shared office. Zane displayed crossed referenced information on the wallscreen for everyone to see clearly.

Zane blinked. "Here's the oldest cross reference between the former police captain and Cipher. There was a dummy company run by Cliff. There's a Jessa that was in on it."

Zeta said, "Oh, that was the case that involved me. I was working for the murder victim. He knew just before the murder took place and he told me to run. He didn't want anything bad to happen to me."

Julian smiled. "I suppose he didn't know you couldn't run and I caught you."

Zeta nodded. "That's the one. It had something to do with robots and androids."

Zelda said, "Zeta's work she did for the deceased helped us solve the case."

Zane nodded. "Okay, that was one."

Zanthe said, "I remember reading the book. That was when Zelda and Julian met Zeta."

Zelda smiled and nodded. "It was. Julian had some trouble and was afraid he was falling for the prime suspect. We were both relieved when Zeta's innocence was proven. She just worked for the deceased and had no idea of the rivalry with Cliff."

Zeta said, "It was a shock to me. I didn't get that close to my client. I just hope he liked what I wrote about him."

Zane said, "I'm sure he was happy about it." He paused as he and Zanthe looked over more data. "Here's the next cross reference. This time it's the case I helped you with."

Julian said, "We asked for help and you came."

Zane continued, "It had to do with Paul, Zanthe's half brother, and Curt. All are werewolves."

Zanthe said, "I read the book and Paul told me about it too. Like me, he had no idea until after he had grown up."

Zeta said, "I remember both Zelda and Julian told me they knew they could be fired because they had asked the Guardians for help, but catching a werewolf was out of their league. I'm glad they asked for help."

Zane said, "I still believe they did the right thing."

Zanthe said, "But that's not what the former police captain or Cipher wanted. They were the ones who were letting Curt come back to Tigerwood. Apparently, he was here before when

Lora was a child. He killed her parents and she saw it, but he didn't have time to get her."

Zane said, "So, he was given another opportunity and a job to take out someone else too. The former captain didn't want to stop the werewolf."

Julian said, "I see why he didn't want us to solve that case. It appears he and Cipher wanted an assassin."

Zelda said, "And we got rid of him."

Zane said, "Curt is still in holding. He refuses to repent and become a better person."

Zanthe said, "So, Zane took the bad werewolf away and helped my brother adjust to being one."

Zane smiled. "He's doing much better and Lora is happy with him."

Zanthe smiled. "She is. She told me it was because she knew Paul so well that she was able to accept him as a werewolf."

Zane blinked. "And here's another one involving Sheila who was a zombie master."

Zeta nodded. "That was the first case Xenocryst had. The detectives had just been fired and we formed the agency so they could keep working. I showed them the vandalism happening in restaurants and the police weren't doing anything."

Zelda smiled. "Because the police captain didn't want them to. They shrugged it off as mere vandalism, but Zeta knew it was something more."

Zane said, "Cipher knew Sheila and her abilities. So, it wasn't hard to get back at a rival restaurant."

Julian said, "Cipher has a serious thing with revenge."

Zanthe said, "No kidding. He used to work for the restaurant chain that Sheila was destroying with her zombie crew."

Zeta said, "That case was when I found out what my uncle Xavier was up to. It was good for me that he gave me the property. I didn't have to lose my home because of him and his bad behavior."

Zane nodded. "And you didn't have to lose your friends either."

Zanthe asked, "I read the book and got the impression it was a shock to you to learn what Xavier did."

Zeta sighed. "It was. He was so secretive and I thought he cared about me. I guess I'll never know if he did or not. He was there for me when my parents had died. But he wasn't that close to me even then."

Zelda said, "Zeta, that's not your fault. You're more resilient than Xavier ever gave you credit for."

Zeta said, "I know that now."

Zane said, "Here's another cross reference. Cynthia and Peter."

Zeta sighed. "Peter was my cousin and son of my uncle Xavier."

Zane nodded. "They worked with Cipher and the former police captain."

Zeta sighed. "Of course they did. Seems like Xavier liked that sort of work."

Zane nodded. "So, again you called the Guardians and Sam and Felicia showed up for you."

Zelda said, "I'm glad they did."

Julian said, "So am I. I don't see how we could have gotten through that case without them."

Zanthe asked, "Wasn't it after that case you hired Jaema to take care of your communications?"

Zeta nodded. "Yeah, that's when she was called for an interview and hired. She's a great friend."

Zane said, "Here's another one. It had to do with Wally killing children. His girlfriend Willow killed him and had to spend some time in the mental hospital with his identical twin Waldo."

Zeta said, "Yes, I remember that. Wally mutilated those poor kids. Willow managed to save the last one from death. Did they ever recover from the trauma?"

Zane said, "They are growing up and getting plastic surgery that Waldo pays for out of the inheritance he received from his brother."

Zeta blinked. "Wow, that's kind of Waldo to do that."

Zane said, "He's on the record stating he felt he was obligated to the kid to help out. He didn't want the kid to be shunned by others for scars which aren't their fault."

Julian said, "That makes sense to me."

Zelda said, "At least Willow and Waldo got help afterwards."

Zane said, "They recovered well and fell in love."

Zeta smiled. "They're still together now."

Zelda asked, "So, was Wally working with Cipher and the former police captain?"

Zane nodded. "Yes, he was. His victims were children of Cipher and the police captain's enemies."

Zeta sighed. "Is there more data?"

Zanthe answered, "Yes, there's more. We're not done yet. We just wanted to see how much you have stopped already and see if the recent body dumped in the woods is another case related to Cipher and the former police captain."

Zane said, "Alright, let's move on to the Everything Mega Super Store."

Zeta said, "Those poor penguins. I'm glad they are happy with Tom looking after them."

Zane nodded. "Todd was behind the snowpeople and the oppression of the penguins."

Zelda said, "And he worked with Cipher and the police captain."

Zane said, "Yes, he did."

Zeta blinked. "He used to date Willow. She certainly wasn't surprised it was him behind the store."

Zanthe said, "Todd was one of the people behind the store, but not the only one. Cipher and the police captain started that one too. Todd was the store manager and the visible person in that structure."

Julian said, "I see that now. So, what's next for cross referencing?"

Zane answered, "Next, we find out what Daren, the former police captain, was really into and how he claimed not to believe in weres or vampires."

Zelda said, "Yet, he worked with Cipher. Does that mean he was lying to cover his tracks?"

Zanthe raised an eyebrow. "I think it does mean that. There are lots of references to weres as hit men and witches causing distractions."

Julian said, "Great. So, he lied to us to hide what he was up to."

Zelda said, "And we were too smart for our own good when we solved each case."

Zeta said, "This case was the one with the snowpeople and penguins was when we met Eugenia who has an ability to talk to ghosts."

Zane nodded. "It's an ability she shared with her great aunt Frankie. I wouldn't be surprised if Eugenia can see the ghosts too. She ended up working for Howard who was working closely with Daren and Cipher."

Zeta said, "Then she was fired because she knew things she wasn't supposed to. I'm glad we saved her."

Everyone agreed.

Zane said, "And this leads us to the case with Alara and Oliver. Alara was stood up at the altar."

Zelda said, "I remember because her maid of honor and groom killed his former fiancée. That was a real mess."

Julian said, "That was Jennifer and Lucien who killed the lady and tried to pretend they did nothing. Were they working with Daren and Cipher?"

Zane nodded. "Yes, the former fiancée was in the family that worked against both Daren and Cipher. So, it's a small world."

Zeta asked, "How many more coincidences are there?"

Zane answered, "I don't think many more." He pulled up another case. "I'm sure you remember the Fravel family and the game The One."

Everyone except Zanthe nodded.

Zane continued, "The Fravel family, except for Josephine, worked with Cipher and Daren."

Zelda said, "Of course they did. We solved that with Josephine's help."

Zane nodded. "Okay, then the next case was Charm School. This is where Zanthe comes into play."

Zanthe raised an eyebrow. "We know there was a romance between the founder Ms. Clayborne of Charm School and Cipher. Is there a connection to Helen?"

Zane checked the data and put it on the screen. "Helen had a fling with Daren while married to her husband."

Zeta raised an eyebrow. "Really? Is that all?"

Zane continued, "It was Cipher who made sure Helen would learn about Zanthe's award for protecting the pack and kids."

Zelda said, "Of course. And does that bring us to the last case with the bombs and Nebula?"

Zane nodded. "Yes, it does. Clearly, Cipher was trying to get revenge against a lot of people as we already know."

Zanthe gasped. "Uh, Daren has something against my mother's husband."

Zeta said, "So, another connection."

Zanthe nodded. "I guess Daren believed he was my father."

Zane said, "I think most people assumed that as she was married to him. She was a few months along with you when he died."

Zanthe nodded. "I hope that brings us to the end."

Zane said, "Not quite. We have references to a bank. They are quite vague. I'll send you those and some others which have references to a cult."

Zeta frowned. "So, this current case must be one or the other."

Zelda said, "Then we have another case to do after this current one to clean up the rest of Daren and Cipher's mess."

Zane nodded. "Yes. Just two more. I just hope Zanthe and I can still get married without loss of life or limb."

Julian said, "We are all hoping that."

Zelda studied the data. "Well, I'm not sure which one it could be. With what we've learned about the body, it's not clear why they died. So, that leaves this bank and witchcraft. That cult sounds pretty weird. They seem to believe they can get secrets from the dead."

Zeta said, "Eugenia could be in trouble if the cult finds out about her."

Zanthe said, "Zane, you mentioned her great aunt Frankie had the same ability, so that's something that runs in their family. Does Eugenia have any family we need to be concerned about?"

Zane raised an eyebrow and checked the databases. "She does have family still living. Not a very close connection, but there's this little family related to her." He put their pictures on the screen. "As you can see this couple with their young daughter."

Zelda blinked. "That girl looks related to Eugenia. Perhaps a younger version."

Zanthe said, "In that case, we'll have to look out for that family, especially the girl. I just wish we knew more about the bank." She sighed. "What does this mean? 'They'll love what we will use for collateral. How many people believe they have souls?'"

Everyone puzzled over that information.

Chapter 5 Nightmare

Willow was asleep dreaming and fully aware she was doing so. She found herself walking down a dark corridor. The light was quite dim. The further she walked, the more dread she felt. She didn't know where she was and how long the corridor was.

It was silent when she had started her long walk, but the further along she got, the more she could hear other people talking. The talking was faint and wasn't understandable. Finally, she reached the end of the corridor where there was a closed and locked door.

She stopped and stared at the door. The talking still wasn't understandable, but she felt intense dread and fear. She could hear some screaming as well. She raised her right hand and reached for the doorknob.

As soon as she touched the doorknob, the talking made perfect sense to her. The screaming was loud and intense. She felt herself being drawn into the sealed room.

"Why did I sign that contract?"

"Why did I take my soul for granted?"

"Why did I need that loan?"

"Why did I think it was the right thing to do?"

"Why couldn't I have learned to live within my means?"

Willow felt a dark and malicious entity reaching out for her. It was hungry and smiled at her. Another victim. This one quite willing and wanting to help the trapped ones. The malicious entity keep getting closer. The others screamed one at a time and then in unity.

"The monster is back!"

"Take cover!"

"Where?"

"We all exposed!"

"It's too late for us!"

The trapped souls huddled together. They pushed back on Willow to set her free. She screamed and thrashed in the bed she shared with Waldo. She accidentally hit him and he woke up.

"Willow? What's wrong?" He sat up. "Wake up, Willow!"

She woke up drenched in sweat. She breathed hard. "I heard and felt the trapped souls again. There was a malicious entity going after them."

His eyes widened. "That again. There's something off about that bank."

"I know. I need to tell Xenocryst and Zane. They have to know about it."

"Wait a minute." He grabbed her tablet and handed it to her. "You need to write down the dream first."

She focused on her breathing as she accepted the tablet computer. She quickly opened the app she needed and wrote down her dream as fast as she could. She was still sweating as she recorded every detail of it.

    Waldo got up out of bed and walked to the altar they shared. He lit the sage stick again and breathed deeply as he closed his eyes. He opened them moments later and used the sage stick to purify the house. He made his way around the whole house. He went into the bedroom last.

    There Willow was still recording all the details. She sighed when she had finished and set the tablet on the nightstand. She smelled the sage and tried to relax. He approached her and waved the sage around her. She breathed deeply and closed her eyes.

    Her heart stopped racing. She kept focused on her breathing.

    "I hope this helps."

    "It is helping. I just don't know why I keep getting drawn back to the trapped souls."

    "Perhaps we need to do something about it."

    "Well, I need to contact Xenocryst and Zane. We can work with them to set those trapped souls free."

    "I think that's a good idea." He waved the sage over her tablet computer and then walked back to the altar. He snuffed out the sage stick and walked back to the bedroom.

    He saw her sending a message to Zane and Xenocryst Agency. He blinked and waited until she was done. She finished her message moments later. She sighed and looked up at him.

    "I sent the message and I don't expect them to answer at this time of night. Perhaps in a few hours. I just wish we knew who we were dealing with. Something seems off about the bank and the trapped souls."

Waldo sighed. "I know when we work with them, we do solve things and save people. I'm sure we'll do it again."

"I do hope so. This is the worse thing so far."

"And we both thought what my brother did was terrible."

"It was and still is. How is the survivor doing?"

He blinked. "Her parents keep sending me pictures. She's starting to look more normal. So, the treatments must be working."

"I hope so. I hope what we send her helps her too."

"It probably is."

She smiled at him in the darkness. "I did set the intentions that she would be able to find her true beauty and not have people falling for her because of her looks, but rather for who she is."

He smiled back at her. "I do occasionally get messages from her and she tells me she feels more comfortable in her body now. So, I'm sure your spells are working. She does like the way your skin products smell and feel on her skin. She's a bit nervous about adolescence."

"Can't say I blame her after what's happened to her."

"She does have a few scars left. She's afraid the other adolescents will shun her. I told her if they did, they weren't worth much."

She chuckled softly. "Good for you." She reached out for him. She put her arms around his neck. "Has she seen you?"

"I don't try to get near her. I'm afraid I'd scare her." He slipped his arms around her waist.

"I can't say I blame you. Has she asked?"

"She has asked to meet me. So, I told her that I was the identical twin to the monster who attacked her. She was shocked and said she wasn't sure she could see me. She still thanks me for the support with the care she's needed. I told her it was the least I could do with what I had inherited from him. I figured she needed that money more than I did."

"That's so true."

They kissed and tumbled onto the bed.

The next morning Jaema frowned at the latest message from Willow. She blinked and looked around her tiny home for her dear wife. Zelda was sipping some coffee and looking out the window at Zeta and Julian dancing in the yard.

Jaema sighed and Zelda turned her head to look at her.

"What's wrong, Jaema?"

"Willow sent us another message about trapped souls. She thinks it's important. I don't understand it."

Zelda raised an eyebrow. "We do have a mysterious case to deal with. After cross referencing the data left behind by Daren and Cipher, we know we just have two more cases to deal with. One is a mysterious bank and the other is a cult."

Jaema said, "I see. Well, Willow did mention a bank in her first message and this latest one too."

Zelda blinked. She looked out the window again. "That has to be a clue. Willow knows more about souls and the spirit realm than we do. I think we better listen." She finished her coffee and rinsed out the mug. "If she didn't tell Zane, send him what she sent us."

Jaema blinked. "She sent it to us and to Zane both."

"Good." Zelda stepped outside. "Julian, I think we have a lead on the case."

Julian and Zeta stopped dancing and let go of each other. Zeta blinked.

Julian asked, "What is it now?"

"A message from Willow about trapped souls and something about the new bank in town."

Zeta gasped. "They're trapping souls at the bank."

Jaema stepped outside. "This case has just gotten really creepy."

Zeta took a deep breath. "I don't know how I know that, but it feels true."

Julian nodded. "Your gift might be getting stronger."

Zeta shrugged. "I guess so. It feels so creepy. Like being trapped in a tomb for too long."

Zelda bit her lip. "Willow sent the same message to Zane, so he and Zanthe know too. Perhaps we need to send a decoy to the bank to see what it's all about."

Julian asked, "Who should we send?"

Zeta frowned. "Me."

Everyone looked at her.

Jaema asked, "Is that a good idea?"

Zeta sighed. "I'd know if there were trapped souls in the bank. Didn't you say Willow noticed when she walked past it and around it?"

Jaema nodded.

"Then I should know if I'm inside. I doubt my gift is as strong as hers is. I am curious if the bank has a better deal than what I currently have."

Julian asked, "Are you unhappy with your current bank?"

Zeta shrugged. "I don't know. I've been with them for a long time and I'm not sure if I should stay with them or go with someone else."

Julian sighed. "Alright. Then go to the bank and see what they have to offer. Your pretense is real and that will make it harder for them to tell you're a decoy. Zelda, we should put one of our small scanners on her."

Zelda nodded. "That would be a good idea. I don't want anything to happen to Zeta and the scanner can give us some more information that will also be concrete."

Zeta nodded. "Very well, I'll have the scanner on me. I hope you have one small enough that would be hidden on me."

Zelda said, "I've got one like that and so does Julian."

Julian said, "That's how I learned Zeta's identity. It's in the house."

Zeta followed her husband inside the house they shared. "Jul, are you okay with me doing this?"

He sighed. "I have mixed feelings about it. I trust you and Zane about your ability, but I'm afraid you could get hurt if you do this. You do tend to throw up whenever animals are in distress."

"I know and then Zelda thinks I'm pregnant."

He smiled. "It's interesting that she thinks that. I take it she really cares about you."

"I know she does. She thinks of me as her sister and you as her brother."

His smile got bigger. "I never knew that. Somehow I'm not surprised. We've always been a good team."

"She told me when you first started working together, she was nervous you'd find her attractive. Then she relaxed when she realized you saw her as a person."

"Yeah, I remember that. Some of the other guys were disappointed to learn she's a lesbian, but I never cared. When we met, I looked up her record and discovered she was intelligent and intuitive. I knew we'd get along and solve hard cases together."

"And you still are doing that together."

"Well, we do it with more people now and it gets interesting."

She blinked. "It's funny. I never knew the Guardians were real. I had heard the stories and wanted to believe in them. Then I met Zane and knew they were indeed real."

"I think there are still some who believe them to be a myth. I'm glad they aren't."

"He's going to marry Zanthe soon. I'm excited for them."

He found the little scanner and pinned it on her shirt. "People might think that's jewelry."

"So, you're giving me jewelry now?"

He chuckled. "I'd give you some if I knew you wanted it."

"Just checking."

"How are your legs these days?"

"They feel fine. Jaema and I still exercise together."

"That's good. Can you run if you need to?"

She shrugged. "I haven't tried running yet. I suppose if I needed to, I could for a bit. I don't know how long I could keep it up."

"Okay. That's good enough. Please be careful." He kissed her cheek.

"I will. This isn't the first time I've been in danger."

"I know, but I'm still worrying. I won't be there with you and don't know how fast I'll be able to get to you if you do run into any trouble."

"Understood. I have my wit and that can help me in a bind."

"If your wit fails, then please run as fast and as far as you can."

"I will."

Chapter 6 Another Body

Eugenia received the delivery of the two bodies without complaint. Just acknowledgement of delivery. She used her anti-grav unit to transfer the bodies to the prepping area. She sighed as she looked over their arrangements. She blinked and studied the bodies.

It was oddly quiet. "Have I lost my ability to talk to ghosts?"

Frankie appeared next to her. "Have you? Can you hear me, Eugenia?"

"Yes, Frankie."

"Then you haven't lost your ability."

"But I'm not hearing or seeing any ghosts from these two bodies."

Frankie blinked. "Neither am I."

The live woman and ghost woman looked at each other.

Frankie said, "I can see why you thought you had lost your ability. This is odd and creepy these two bodies don't have ghosts nearby. Give me a some time. I'm going to ask some of the other ghosts if they know." She floated away.

Eugenia sighed. She went to work cleaning and dressing the bodies while she waited for Frankie to come back. The work seemed to take a long time. Eugenia didn't care. She just focused on the work at hand while she missed guidance from the ghosts.

She sighed and looked over their individual requests. Then she worked on one at a time to get the bodies ready for their services. She did see a note for each body from the coroner stating and unknown cause of death.

Eugenia frowned when she saw those notes. She knew something was wrong. As she was finishing up her work, Frankie came back.

"Eugenia, I checked with the other ghosts and they don't know where these ghosts are."

Eugenia blinked. "What?"

Frankie continued, "Some of the ghosts I talked with knew these people and tried to reach them in our realm. There was no response."

Eugenia nodded. "I see. I need to tell Zane about this. Perhaps it will help the case." She wasted no time calling.

"Are you done prepping these bodies?" asked Frankie.

"Yes."

"Hi, Eugenia. We were hoping you'd have some information on the dead."

Eugenia sighed. "Zane, there's no ghosts and for a minute I was afraid I'd lost my ability. Then Frankie showed up. She couldn't see the ghosts either. She left while I prepared the bodies to check in her realm to see what she could learn."

Zane gasped. "Those bodies don't have ghosts?"

Eugenia said, "No ghosts here. Frankie said she found some

ghosts who knew them while they were alive and no one knows where these ghosts are now."

Zane sighed. "I think Willow knows where they are."

Eugenia asked, "Is that the Willow who killed her boyfriend because he was mutilating children and killing them?"

"The very same. This current case has to do with the new bank in town."

Eugenia sighed. "So, these missing ghosts are trapped. That would explain why no other ghost around here can find them."

Frankie sighed. "They could be trapped inside the bank. I heard some of the ghosts talk about how eerie that building is. They feel repulsed by it. They said something about a monster there that like to eat souls." She shivered.

Eugenia gaped. "Uh, Zane, Frankie just mentioned what some of the ghosts are saying about that bank."

Zane said, "Oh?"

Eugenia continued, "The ghosts say they are repulsed by it and think there are trapped souls inside with a monster who likes to eat souls."

Zane sighed. "Willow has nightmares about the same thing. She wants to help set those souls free."

Frankie said, "I'm glad Willow is on our side. I'd worry if she was harming people. I was shocked to learn she killed her boyfriend until I learned the reason. I can rally up the other ghosts to help those trapped souls once they are free."

Eugenia said, "Zane, Frankie says she can rally the other ghosts to help once the trapped souls are free."

Zane said, "We can use all the help we can get. For now, we're looking for concrete proof. What we have so far is what Willow has learned and what you two just found out. Both match, so we're on the right track."

Eugenia asked, "Will someone have to visit the bank?"

Zane answered, "Yes, I believe Zeta will do so. If you feel like doing so too, it's not a bad idea. I know you can hear the ghosts."

Eugenia said, "I think it would be a good idea for me to check it out. Perhaps I can go when Zeta does. Frankie, will you come too? You don't have to get inside. Just let me know what you discover when we're there."

Frankie sighed. "For you, I will go there and I won't promise I'll go inside. Most places aren't so bad to visit as a ghost, but this bank is not something I'm sure of. I don't know if we can get inside without getting trapped."

Eugenia said, "Okay, Zane, Frankie has agreed to come with me, but she isn't promising she will try to get inside of the bank. She isn't sure it's safe and I agree with her."

Zane said, "In that case, please coordinate with Zeta when you go and what you will do once there. This case is certainly creepy as the others I'm working with say."

Eugenia said, "I would tend to agree and I'm used to talking with ghosts. I missed doing that while I prepared these bodies. I just hope I did what they wanted. I had to guess this time and usually I don't have to."

Zane said, "So, you can just ask when they are there with you."

Eugenia nodded. "Exactly. The ghosts do make my job so much easier. I wouldn't be surprised if these bodies died without souls living in them."

Zane said, "That would be my guess too. Anything else you need to tell me?"

Eugenia looked at Frankie who shook her head no.

"No, that's it from Frankie and me."

Zane said, "Good. I'll let you coordinate with Zeta for the next step in the case."

They disconnected and Eugenia sighed. She looked at her aunt. "Frankie, I don't like this, but something is seriously wrong. I know we can do something more than prepare the dead for their services."

"We certainly can. Call Zeta and I'll go talk with the other ghosts. I think it will take more of us to stop this threat."

Eugenia called Zeta through Xenocryst. Jaema connected them immediately.

Zeta said, "Hi, Eugenia. This is a surprise."

Eugenia said, "I just talked to Zane after I had just finishing prepping the two bodies that no one is sure how they died." She sighed. "Their ghosts weren't here and the other ghosts couldn't find them either. We're thinking they might be trapped in the bank."

Zeta said, "Oh! That's what Willow has been saying with her dreams and impressions of the bank. Do you want to come to the bank with me?"

Eugenia closed her eyes. "Yes, I think it's a good idea. If there are any trapped ghosts in there, I should be able to hear them."

Zeta said, "In that case, the more the merrier. I can sense what others feel, but can't communicate with them. I'm still learning."

Eugenia opened her eyes. "Your gift might be somewhat different from mine. My aunt Frankie will come too. She isn't promising she will try to get inside, but she will at least observe the bank from the outside."

Zeta said, "That's good. I know we can use help from the local ghosts. I just hope they don't get trapped too."

Frankie reappeared. "That's good to hear, Zeta."

Eugenia said, "Frankie just came back and she's glad to hear you say that."

Zeta said, "I was planning to see what options they have with accounts and so on. I'm not sure I'm entirely happy with my current bank. I know that will help out while I'm there."

Eugenia blinked. "I could do the same. Perhaps see what the loan options are."

Zeta said, "That would be good. Willow mentioned there was

something about contracts and loans that were broken."

Eugenia said, "Then I think we're on to something."

Frankie said, "Some of the other ghosts want to come too. They wonder if the missing ghosts are there in the bank."

Eugenia blinked. "Frankie says other ghosts will come with us to see if the missing ghosts are there."

Zeta said, "I appreciate the help. I will have a scanner on me too to help with more data."

Eugenia said, "Even better. I know whatever your scanner picks up will be helpful and can back up our impressions."

Zeta said, "My husband is afraid for me to do this. I think he will be happy to know you'll be there."

Frankie said, "We'll look after you, Zeta."

Eugenia smiled. "Frankie said she and the other ghosts will look after you. I will too."

Zeta said, "I can look after you too, Eugenia."

"Thank you."

Zeta said, "So, I suppose we could just use our real identities. I tend to be in the background of the agency."

Eugenia nodded. "I think that should be fine. The more truth we interject into our roles, the harder it will be for them to understand what we are really up to."

Zeta said, "It will be easier to remember as well."

Eugenia said, "I just hope they don't figure it out until we are away."

Zeta said, "I've read posts on social media about the bank. I don't see any bad or critical reviews. Just raving about how good they are. Oh, and I see the two dead contributed too. That has to be a clue."

Eugenia said, "So, they got something for giving a good review, but if their souls are trapped in the bank, then that must be the reason their bodies died. Physical bodies can't live without souls."

Zeta said, "I would imagine that to be true. Do you think we need anything else to prepare?"

Eugenia answered, "Hmm. I don't think so. I think we're ready. We know our information and that helps out quite a bit."

Zeta asked, "Do we need to ask other questions unrelated to our initial queries?"

Eugenia answered, "I'm not sure that's a good idea. I think we just stick to our queries. That way they aren't as likely to get suspicious of us than if we ask other questions."

Zeta said, "Okay, then I think we're all set on that part. When would you like to go?"

"How about tomorrow?"

"That shouldn't be a problem for me. What time?"

They picked the time and added the event to their calendars. They disconnected and Zeta let her husband know of the modified plan. Eugenia sighed.

Frankie looked at her. "This is a scary mission."

Eugenia nodded. "Zeta will probably get sick if there are trapped souls in that bank."

Frankie sighed. "We know she does that. That woman has quite a bit of empathy. She's quite sensitive even if she can't hear us talking."

Eugenia blinked. "So, I may have to help her get out of there, if things get bad."

Frankie nodded. "You just might. I think we'll get Willow to be there around the same time to help out."

Eugenia said, "Very well. We can use all the support we can get for this."

Frankie asked, "Are you ready for tomorrow?"

"I've prepared as much as I can."

"I know you know what questions to ask and get the basic information, but are you mentally prepared?"

Eugenia blinked and then sighed. "I don't know. It's quite eerie not to be able to talk with ghosts while I was preparing their bodies. We need to know if there are souls trapped inside that bank. Then we will have to figure out a way to set them free."

Frankie smiled. "Good. Now I know you are ready."

Chapter 7 Decoys

Julian sighed. "Are you sure you want to do this, Zeta?"

She nodded. "Yes, I want to learn more about this special bank. There are people on social media who rave how wonderful it is. I could just say I'm there to see if I can get a better deal than what I currently get." She put on the scanner as a piece of jewelry as he had done the day before.

He sighed again. "Very well. Just be careful."

"I will. I'm not going alone as I originally planned. Eugenia is coming with me. She's going to ask similar questions."

He smiled. "That does help out a little bit. I'm still nervous."

"Eugenia said Frankie and other ghosts will come to see what they can learn. I have your scanner on me now. I'm sure we'll learn something from going there."

"Alright." He picked up his tablet computer. "The scanner is still working. It will tell me where you are."

"That's fine." She kissed him goodbye and walked out of their house. She said goodbye to both Zelda and Jaema before passing through the gate.

Her legs were doing well. She took a deep breath and relaxed as much as she could. She knew she needed to be calm in order for this enquiry to turn out well. The point was to get more information and to discover if there were trapped souls inside the bank.

She sighed and soon she was joined in her walk by Eugenia.

"I'm a bit nervous too, Zeta."

"Hi, Eugenia. I hope I don't get sick again."

"So do I. I understand you can sense others' distress. Have you ever heard ghosts talking?"

Zeta shook her head. "No, I didn't pick up on any language messages from the penguins or the wolves. I just thought if there were trapped souls in the bank as Willow says, I would feel their pain. That would confirm what she's been telling us."

Eugenia sighed. "I'll be able to hear them talking or screaming as the case may be."

"Right. You said Frankie and other ghosts would be there. I don't know if they are here now."

Eugenia blinked. "None are around us right now. They'll meet us at the bank even though it bothers them."

Zeta sighed. "I'm glad they are helping. I could use the moral support. I just need to stick to the plan. I'm looking for what they offer and then I can compare it to what I currently have."

Eugenia said, "That works for me. If I do discover any ghosts inside the bank, I can talk to them without moving my mouth."

"That's good. I'm sure that will help us out."

They stopped as soon as they could see the bank. They frowned and stared at it. It loomed over the pedestrian traffic. They turned their heads to look at each other. Their frowns disappeared and they nodded to each other.

They started walking again and entered the bank. The inside of the bank looked quite ordinary. There weren't any paintings or anything special decorating it. It was stark and boring. Yet, there were plenty of people coming and going doing their banking business.

Eugenia and Zeta stared all around them. It was quite large for a bank. Perhaps larger than it needed to be. It was certainly larger than the original bank that used to be in the same spot.

"Welcome. May I help you?"

Eugenia and Zeta blinked and looked at a well dressed lady smiling at them.

"Are you interested in opening any accounts with us today?"

Zeta recovered first. "I was looking for information on what kinds of accounts you offer."

Eugenia felt sick in the pit of her stomach. "Yes, I was wondering about personal and business accounts."

"You've come to the right place. As you can see..." She swept her hand in the air to point out all the happy customers. "We have lots of happy customers already. They know they are getting good deals on their accounts."

Zeta blinked and something felt off about the happy customers. There was something dark and sinister just beyond the walls of the lobby. She wasn't sure what it was. All she knew was that she could feel it. "Are there any fees involved with your accounts?"

"No, unreasonable fees. We have overdraft protections and loans to help you afford whatever extravagant dreams you have."

Zeta blinked. "I see. That sounds pretty good."

Eugenia heard screaming from just beyond them in the lobby. No one else heard it. "I see. So, with the overdraft protections, does that mean you will allow transactions to go through even when the money isn't in our accounts?"

The lady laughed. "How cute. You think we'd take advantage of you? We don't do that here. If you don't have enough money, then we will loan it to you. It's a complimentary service we offer for no extra fee."

Zeta raised an eyebrow. "Really? What if we don't want that? What if we want the charge to bounce instead of going through?"

The lady blinked. "Why would you want to do that? Don't you want to live your wildest dreams? There is more to this life than just ordinary and mundane concerns. We all deserve to live the good life."

Zeta felt nauseous. She knew something was wrong. Too many nearby were in distress and the fear was mounting. She could feel the vomit rising from inside. She focused on her breathing.

Eugenia kept hearing screaming. More and louder. She knew it was coming from the vault. "What do you use for collateral for your loans?"

The lady smiled. "Your soul, which isn't a real thing. So, it's no big deal if you can't pay off your loans."

Eugenia saw Zeta's skin get paler. "My friend and I will have to think about it."

"Why not sign up right now?"

Eugenia didn't hesitate as she took Zeta by the arm. "We have to leave now. We might be back later."

"Don't take too long. See you soon." The lady kept smiling as if she was on botox.

Eugenia gently tugged Zeta out of the bank. Outside the sun was shining as if nothing was wrong. They said nothing as they walked around towards the back of the bank. There Frankie and other ghosts were standing nearby.

"Eugenia, don't let go of Zeta." Frankie looked at the pale elf. "This bank is as bad as the ghosts said it was."

Eugenia sighed. "I heard some ghosts screaming in the vault. There's a monster in there who likes to eat them."

The ghosts gasped.

Frankie said, "One of the ghosts was brave enough to get inside and they disappeared. We haven't heard from them since."

Eugenia sighed. Zeta threw up.

Eugenia said, "I wouldn't be surprised if that was who I heard screaming in the lobby. There are quite a few screaming in the vault."

Willow blinked and stopped near everyone. "That's what I've discovered too."

Zeta sighed. "Willow, you're right. They are trapped inside that horrible place. Too many can't get out because of bad contracts."

Willow said, "They pushed me out."

Eugenia said, "They probably could push you out because you still have a physical body. Frankie, did that ghost who went inside have a contract with the bank?"

Frankie blinked. "I doubt it. They were dead before the bank was here."

Eugenia said, "The bank sets up the accounts so that you can keep spending until your account is empty and they just give you the loan with your soul as collateral. It's so disgusting and creepy."

Zeta said, "So, not a better deal than what I currently have."

Frankie said, "Just keep breathing, Zeta."

Zeta focused on her breathing and felt supported by those around her.

Willow said, "So, how do we break them out of there?"

Frankie answered, "We don't know. We're not going in there if we can't get out."

Willow said, "We won't ask you to. Perhaps we need to do a shamanic journey and find a way to break them out."

Zeta straightened up. "I should go with you on that journey."

Eugenia sighed. "Won't that be dangerous?"

Willow answered, "It doesn't have to be dangerous. Waldo and I will set up a safe way to do so. Zeta, you are welcome to join us. Have you done one before?"

Zeta shook her head. "No, I just know it's a good idea. I can't tell how many are trapped inside."

Willow nodded. "I can't tell either."

Eugenia blinked. "I know I can't tell. All I can tell you is that they are inside the vault."

Zeta said, "I wonder how they managed to stay in business if they don't have fees."

Willow said, "They must get their money from somewhere else."

Zeta said, "So, perhaps this is a front for something else?"

No one else said anything. The ghosts talked among themselves to see if they could help with the journey to the vault.

After several moments had gone by, Frankie said, "We think we have something which could help. Willow, do you know what the monster hates?"

Willow blinked. "No. What is it?"

Frankie answered, "The ghost who went in told us when they were in the wall that the monster hates cinnamon."

Willow smiled. "We can use plenty of cinnamon around us."

Zeta blinked. "What's wrong with cinnamon?"

Eugenia answered, "Nothing to most of us, but this monster

apparently does have a serious problem with it."

Zeta blinked. "So, we did learn some things about this bank. They do use souls as collateral for loans you don't even have to ask for. Just be irresponsible with your money and keep spending it."

Eugenia said, "The monster who likes to eat souls can't stand cinnamon. So, you'll need lots of it for your shamanic journey into the bank."

Willow said, "And we need to stay alive so we don't get trapped."

Zeta blinked. "We can call in the werewolves and the detectives to help with physical protection. Willow, I'm sure you and Waldo know plenty of ways to protect yourself spiritually."

Willow nodded. "So, now we need to all get together and plan this with the others."

Eugenia said, "I don't think I'm of anymore use to the case."

Zeta said, "If anyone else dies, you have to take care of their bodies."

Eugenia said, "This is true and I don't mind that part. I just prefer to do that work with the ghosts guiding me. It was eerie when they weren't around. I did my best and hope it will be fine with them."

Zeta said, "I'm sure whatever you did is fine. You are good at your job. You've done it enough to know what needs to be done and how to guess."

Eugenia nodded. "You're right, but it still bothers me. It's just easier when I can ask the ghosts especially if they don't leave any instructions before they die."

Willow said, "We need to leave the area. Someone is coming out of the bank and they look official."

Zeta and Eugenia followed Willow out of the area. The ghosts all disappeared and went elsewhere. Willow, Zeta and Eugenia kept walking and were quiet for some time until they had reached a safe area.

Willow said, "Zeta, if you don't mind, I want to walk to your place before I go home."

Zeta blinked. "Okay, that's fine. Eugenia, are you coming with us?"

Eugenia shook her head. "I think I better get home and check my schedule. I know I have two services coming up soon."

Zeta said, "Good luck with those."

Eugenia smiled and went her way while Willow and Zeta walked to her home. They entered the gate and Zeta let Jaema know what she and Willow had decided to do next. There the werewolves were contacted and the arrangements were made.

It was time to bring all the different clues together out in the open and see what more they could do about the bank. The detectives waited and gathered up what they knew for now. There was more information on the bank than what they had originally thought.

Zeta and Willow talked more about shamanic journey while they waited for everyone to show up with their individual parts. Jaema continued to monitor all communications and wonder what would happen once they were able to open the case wide open.

Chapter 8 Connections

Jaema and Zelda sat next to each other as Zeta lit the firepit. She sat down next to Julian. Soon Zane and Zanthe came and sat down next to each other. A moment later, Willow and Waldo sat down in the remaining two seats which were next to each other. Everyone was thoughtful as they stared into the fire.

Zanthe said, "Zane and I were able to get the bank records from the decreased without ghosts. They had accounts at the new bank."

Zane continued, "They had overdrawn their accounts and were given the loans without asking for them."

Zeta said, "We were told how that worked, but the over enthusiastic lady didn't explain the catch to those loans very well." She paused to take a deep breath. "She mentioned our souls are the collateral and they weren't real. So, we have nothing to really lose."

Willow sighed. "So, they are trapped in the bank with others."

Zanthe said, "I think it's quite clear what's happened and I can see why some people would go along with it. They must not believe in souls and how we need to take care of ours."

Willow blinked. "I can see why it sounds too good to be true. When do the loans come due?"

Zane answered, "From what we can tell, there is a grace period and then when the loans have to be paid back, but the deceased were so in debt they didn't have a chance to pay them back."

Zanthe said, "That's what the records say. They died not long after their loans came due."

Julian nodded. "So, our next step should be for Zelda and I to go into the bank and question the CEO and see if we can learn what happened to them."

Willow said, "We can guess the deceased went to the bank to see if anything else could be done and their souls were taken. Their physical bodies died after that."

Zane nodded. "It's all so logical, but I doubt the police will believe it or even view it as a form of murder."

Zanthe sighed. "But it's enough that we know it. Is there any way we can break those souls out of there and shut down the bank?"

Willow answered, "Zeta, Waldo and I want to go on a shamanic journey surrounded by lots of cinnamon. We would also like Julian and Zelda to be there to protect our physical bodies."

Zelda nodded. "That's not a bad idea. We can do that after we visit the bank."

Julian nodded. "I like that idea. What about the laws concerning banks?"

Zanthe smiled. "Right, I forgot about that. I haven't finished my schooling yet and I know we haven't covered banks. We will soon. I suppose Zane and I can check on the laws for Tigerwood and see how they think they can get away with using souls for collateral. Frankly, I don't see how the bank can be solvent with its practices."

Zane smiled. "Well, we know Cipher and Daren had something to do with the planning stages of this bank. I wouldn't be surprised if they are laundering money. Or even other illegal activities."

Julian smiled. "So, you have a possible lead to look into to shut the bank down."

Willow blinked. "And we will break those trapped souls out of there."

Zanthe said, "It's interesting how this case started. It didn't make any sense at first and even the coroner was puzzled as to how the deceased died. Yet, with all the pieces we have brought together, we know what this case is about and we know how to solve it."

Zelda blinked. "I think when you crossed references the data left behind from both Daren and Cipher with our cases, it helped out a lot. I'm sure we can finish this case, but what about the next one?"

Willow blinked. "There's a next one?"

Zanthe said, "It has to do with a cult and more magic. We'll probably need your expertise on it."

Zeta said, "It might also concern Eugenia too. Or at least a relative of hers."

Willow raised an eyebrow. "I know some abilities run in families. I take it this relative of hers will be wanted by the cult for that ability."

Zane said, "That's what we're thinking, but we have the police monitoring the family. Eugenia's relative is a minor and currently lives with her parents."

Zanthe said, "Nothing out of the ordinary has happened yet. But, if it does, we're calling all of you to help out."

Willow nodded. "Count me in."

Zanthe said, "Now back to our current case. There's been more bodies found and Eugenia reports they have no ghosts with them. Zane and I checked their bank records and it's the same story for all of them."

Zelda said, "Jul, looks like you and I have something we can take care of tomorrow."

Julian nodded. "Yeah, we're going to the bank with our questions. When do you want to do the shamanic journey?"

Willow answered, "We can do it tomorrow night. That seems to be the best and hopefully, you will be free."

Jaema sighed. "This case and the next one both sound creepy to me. I suppose we can solve them just as we have the others. Makes me want to hope we can stick to the boring ones that require us to track cheating partners."

Zeta smiled. "They pay the bills, but they aren't as exciting as these cases are."

Jaema shook her head. "I know that. I don't get why the cult wouldn't want Eugenia for the evil plans."

Zeta blinked. "Perhaps they prefer someone young who would be more malleable."

Zane said, "That's probably it. Eugenia does have a history of not being submissive. Her work history demonstrates that at the bare minimum."

Zanthe bit her lip. "That actually makes sense. I think that's also why it's usually young people who go to college or they get sucked into things which can be beyond them. They think they see a good opportunity, but it could be a scam."

Zelda said, "Anyone can be scammed and tricked, but if you're referring to lack of experience, then yes, that can make a huge difference."

Zanthe nodded. "I think that's what I was thinking. Like when I found out I'm a werewolf and had no idea before it had happened."

Zane said, "You were lucky you were close to the woods when you found out. You had a safe place to shapeshift."

Zanthe said, "That's very true. I take it, it doesn't always work out that well for other weres."

Zane said, "No, some end up transforming in front of others for the first time and everyone gets scared. However, if you grow up in a Guardian Hold, we'll know if it's possible from your DNA and warn you about it before it ever happens."

Zanthe asked, "Have you experienced that?"

"Not me personally. I was able to shapeshift as a child and my parents were with me. They knew what to do. I did grew up with a few other kids who had similar genes. My parents and other weres took them aside to teach them what it could mean. Not all of them ended up with two forms. The ones who did at least knew enough when it started happening to get to the safe place to transform."

Zanthe asked, "Was it still a shock for them?"

Zane nodded. "It was. However, they knew enough to guess what it could be. I remember I helped one to get to the safe area before they fully transformed."

Zelda said, "That sounds scary, but supportive."

Zane nodded. "Yes, we do our best to help those who either don't know and it happened to them. Or we check their DNA first and then give them the talk. Many who had the talk before their transformations were able to cope with it better."

Zanthe said, "I could have used that talk before it happened to me. But I have gotten used to it."

Zane said, "That's why I told you I wasn't going to mentor you. You already had a good hold on it. I think you must have accepted it fairly quickly."

Zanthe smiled. "The pack helped me. They accepted me even though they knew what I was. They explained what they could to me and then I didn't worry about it. It became a part of myself that I had to learn about and explore. So, I had support and I know that makes all the difference in the world."

Willow said, "That does help out. I know I had mentors when I was learning about magic. I was even in a coven at one time. But, like Zanthe, I still had to explore on my own or else I wouldn't know what I know now."

Zeta said, "So, that's why Zane keeps telling me to practice and stay grounded."

Willow smiled. "Zane knows what he's talking about. Grounding is the best thing you can do while you learn how to use your gift. I would hope that you won't get so physically ill while picking up on others' distress."

Zeta said, "That would be great. Every time I do get sick from my gift, Zelda is afraid I'm pregnant. Sometimes she chews out Julian about it."

Zelda said, "Guilty as charged. Well, it would be half his fault."

Julian said, "Of course it would be. I would continue to look after her."

Zeta kissed him on his cheek. "You do such a good job about it."

Willow smiled. "That's sweet. Zeta, if you need mentoring, I'd be happy to do it."

Zeta said, "Thank you, Willow. I just might take you up on it."

Zelda said, "Jul, we need to come up with our questions."

Zane pulled out his tablet computer. "I'm sending you the bank records of the deceased to make it easier for you to do so."

Zelda said, "Thank you. That will definitely help with coming up with questions."

Julian said, "Such as, when was the last time the deceased was in the bank."

Zanthe said, "The bank has cameras and they aren't releasing the footage."

Zane said, "I'm on it. There system is a bit hard to hack into, but in this case, I'm not giving up."

Zeta blinked. "What about asking Nebula to hack into their system?"

Zane smiled. "That's an excellent idea. I wouldn't be surprised if Cipher had something to do with their security system." He sent a message to Nebula and then received one back within moments. "Nebula will do it. He thinks he has a good idea of how to hack in after reading what Cipher knew about it."

Zelda said, "That's a relief. Will the ghosts and that monster show up on the footage?"

Zane blinked. "That's depends upon what kind of cameras they use. If they are the standard ones, then the ghosts and the monster may not show up."

Julian asked, "If they are standard cameras, would Nebula add the ones that would record ghosts?"

Zane send another message to Nebula. "They would be happy to sneak into the bank and do just that. We need to give them some time."

Willow said, "The shamanic journey we will be doing may not free anyone the first time. However, we might be able to find a way to set them free. We just need to talk with the trapped souls first and study the bank itself."

Zane nodded. "I'll let Nebula know. If anyone can get into the bank and study its layout and hack into its system, they can without getting caught."

Zeta smiled. "I'm so glad Nebula is on our side."

Zanthe smiled. "They probably still feel some guilt about the bombs and the people they harmed. I'm just glad they are cooperating and now I know we can solve this case."

Everyone relaxed a bit more as they planned their next steps to gather more information. Nebula smiled at the messages and felt glad they were wanted and needed in something big. It was the least they could do to make things right for others.

Even Ariana was excited about Nebula's new assignment. She encouraged them to do what was necessary and even offered some suggestions as to how to go about some of it.

Chapter 9 The Special Bank

Zelda looked to Julian as they were standing outside of their tiny houses. "Jul, are you ready?"

Julian nodded. "Yeah, let's get this over with. I know my wife, Eugenia and Willow can't be wrong as to what is happening in the new bank."

She nodded. "There's also the evidence that all the deceased had accounts with the bank and all died not long after their loans were due."

"I do hope Nebula was able to hack into their security system and add the special cameras if they're needed."

She blinked. "They were somewhat creepy when they were attempting to seduce Zeta and yet never complained when I shot them to protect her."

"They are a puzzled."

They said goodbye to their wives and left the property through the gate. The sun was shining with a cool breeze. Nothing seemed out of the ordinary. The pedestrian traffic was normal and wasn't a problem for the detectives.

Before they had realized it, they were at the bank. They stopped and looked at the building. It was huge and unimpressive compared to the original bank that was in the same location. They looked at each other and then back at the entrance.

They walked inside and were greeted by a well dressed woman. "Welcome. Are you interested in opening accounts with us?"

Julian answered, "No, we're here to see the CEO of this bank."

The greeter blinked. "Why would you need to see him?"

Zelda answered, "We're Detectives Julian and Zelda. We need to question him about some recent deaths of people who had accounts with your bank."

The greeter frowned. "He's quite busy and doesn't have time to answer questions."

The detectives flashed their badges. The greeter sighed and turned around to look for the CEO.

She turned back around. "Alright, this way."

They followed her to the office on the opposite side of the bank near the vault.

"Knock, knock."

The CEO looked up from his desk. "Yes, dear?"

"Detectives Julian and Zelda would like to talk to you about some people who recently died and had accounts with us."

The CEO blinked. "Detectives, come in. Dear, close the door behind you."

The detectives walked inside the office and the greeter closed the door behind them.

"You really don't think my bank has something to do with

their deaths, do you?"

Julian said, "We're not sure what to think. We just have that connection with the recent deaths."

Zelda said, "How about we give you their names and you can tell us if they came here once their loans were due? We have a list here." She sent it to the CEO's computer.

The CEO blinked. "Yes, I remember all of them. I can give you the records of them coming here." He did so without emotion to her little portable computer.

Zelda looked over the data. "Thank you." She looked at Julian.

Julian said, "That was just before they died. Interesting coincidence."

The CEO smiled. "It's just a coincidence. We had nothing to do with their deaths."

Zelda said, "Even though you used people's souls as collateral?" She smiled like a Cheshire cat.

The CEO chuckled. "Everyone knows that's all nonsense. We don't actually claim their souls when they can't pay their loans. We garnish their wages. I wouldn't be surprised if they all committed suicide when they realized they had no way out of their debt. It's a common thing to see in my business."

Julian said, "Of course it is. We just have to check. So, what was their collateral that you collected from them?"

The CEO frowned. "It says so in the records I just gave you.

Surely you two can read."

Zelda raised an eyebrow. "I don't see anything listed as collateral on their loans. How do you manage to stay in business when you give away free money?"

"I was sure it was listed. I find it hard to believe my people would omit such a thing."

The detectives glanced at each other and then back at the CEO.

Julian said, "I believe there are omissions in the information you just gave us."

"Impossible. I gave you everything you needed to know. I don't doubt for one minute they all committed suicide. We are a solid and legal bank. We have to think about our financial backers and our customers. Nothing else matters."

Zelda asked, "What if they die?"

"Then we close their accounts."

Julian asked, "Do you go after their heirs to get your loan money back?"

"No, why would we do that? That would just be absurd."

Zelda said, "Indeed." She felt her scanner buzz against her. "How many customers do you currently have?"

The CEO blinked. "We have plenty and they keep up with their payments as they should. They understand what the consequences are if they don't."

Julian said, "I would hope you make that clear. If you didn't, there would be lawsuits."

The CEO smiled. "There won't be any lawsuits. We haven't done anything wrong."

Zelda said, "I certainly hope not. However, we still have to check every lead."

The CEO nodded. "Of course. It was all the same with those former customers. They panicked knowing their loans were due and they came in to renegotiate their loans to keep themselves afloat. We made them a better deal and then they left. We didn't see them after that."

Again Zelda's scanner buzzed against her. Julian's did the same a moment later. They didn't glance at each other this time. Instead they tried something else.

Julian asked, "What kind of terms did you give them?"

The CEO blinked. "We extended the deadline so we could garnish their wages. It was all they had left."

Zelda said, "I see. So, nothing about they have to give up their souls or that their heirs will have to pay off the loans once they are confirmed dead?"

"No, of course not. The collateral wasn't really souls. They aren't real. We need something more tangible. We just say that to get people to come up and open accounts with us."

Zelda said, "So, you lure people who don't know much about money into your bank and take advantage of them."

"No, we don't do that. We educate them on how to manage

their finances better. We do that to keep our customers happy and help them plan ahead for whatever they want including retirement."

Julian said, "Interesting. So, the souls as collateral and living your wildest dreams is just a way to lure people in. It sounds too good to be true."

The CEO smiled. "We have them take financial awareness classes. The classes are taught by our experts to teach financial literacy and how to deal with bills and loans. Many of our customers love the classes and recommend their friends and family to us. We are highly rated by our customers. We wouldn't kill them for any reason. It would be stupid as they are the reason we can stay in business."

Zelda looked over the data one more time. "Well, thank for the data and for your time. We have what we need now."

The CEO smiled. "Anything for you, detectives."

Julian opened the door and let Zelda pass through first before leaving the office and closing the door. They said nothing as they left the bank. The greeter stared daggers from a face frozen by botox at their backs.

The detectives stepped outside and walked away from the bank. They walked to the police station to visit the werewolves. They walked into the open office.

Zanthe looked up. "Something didn't go well."

Zelda answered, "No and our scanners picked up things just

as Zeta's did when she was there."

Zane sighed. "What did you find out?"

Zelda answered, "The CEO gave us data on the deceased that I'm not sure it is the correct information. He claimed they just use the promise of unlimited money and souls as collateral as a gimmick to get people to open accounts. Then they give the customers financial literacy classes and pointed out all the good reviews they've received."

Zane nodded. "Which we already knew about the reviews. What did your scanners pick up?"

Zelda sent her data first. Then Julian did the same. Zane put the data on the wallscreen so everyone could see it.

Zanthe said, "I see something is off about the CEO."

Zane nodded. "He must know magic. Perhaps even necromancy. Clearly, he was trying to do something to the two of you."

Zanthe said, "That might be why the questioning went badly. I see the data he sent you doesn't match the data Zane acquired."

Zane said, "I see that clearly. The original contracts state souls are collateral for any complimentary loans they get. And no safeties with those accounts."

Zelda said, "So, where is the money coming from?"

Zanthe said, "That's what we've just discovered. Cipher is dead and Daren is in prison, but we discovered another backer.

Daemon who runs the cult we've been warned about."

Julian asked, "What is the cult's name?"

"Necromancers Who Discover the Secrets of the Dead," answered Zanthe.

Zelda asked, "How dangerous are they?"

Zane said, "We don't know. They don't have any criminal records at all. Not even Daemon."

Julian said, "Great, so there is a cult involved with this mess."

Zanthe said, "Could the CEO be a part of the cult?"

Zane answered, "Yes and he could be the monster Willow, Eugenia and Zeta picked up on."

Zelda asked, "So now what?"

Julian answered, "We need to protect Willow, Waldo and Zeta when they go on their shamanic journey tonight."

Zane said, "We got new data from Nebula."

Zelda asked, "What did they find out?"

Zane answered, "They got into the bank and installed the special cameras and hacked into the security system. It was set up by Cipher."

Zanthe sighed. "I'm glad Nebula is on our side."

Zane continued, "There are lots of trapped souls inside the bank. Nebula wasn't sure who they all were, but figured they were customers of the bank or other souls the necromancers were able to trap inside. Nebula saw the monster too."

Zelda sighed. "What did they think about the monster?"

Zane took a deep breath. "The monster is dangerous and threatens to eat the souls especially if they don't tell him whatever he wants to know."

Julian said, "So, he's a part of the cult."

Zane nodded. "The bank isn't legal either."

Zanthe added, "We've already filed legal actions against it. It's a matter of time before the bank gets shut down."

Zelda said, "Then after we deal with this bank, we have to go after the cult."

Zanthe nodded. "We warned Eugenia. She's worried about her relatives even though they aren't on the best of terms." She paused. "I certainly know how that feels."

Julian asked, "How long will the legal action take?"

Zane blinked. "Shouldn't take long for them to respond to it. Then we can begin to shut them down with hard evidence from their own records."

Zelda nodded. "Good. That's at least something. I just hope the witches can find a way to release the souls."

Zane said, "I don't doubt they will find a way. I know there are ghosts in this city who will be supportive and help out in any way they can."

Julian said, "At this point, we will take all the help we can get even if we can't communicate directly with them."

Zelda asked, "Jul, are you ready to go? I think we better get Zeta and go to Willow and Waldo's."

Julian answered, "Yeah, I'm ready. You two are coming too?" The werewolves smiled.

Zanthe said, "I was hoping to study while we wait for anything out of the ordinary."

Zane said, "I'll be scanning as I'm sure you two will be."

Zelda smiled. "I have my gun. I think we'll be alright. We just need to stand guard to keep the three travelers safe from physical harm."

Zanthe and Zane stood up from their desks and followed the detectives out of the police station. No one said another word about the case. They just walked in silence as they prepared for the night and their roles in the shamanic journeying.

Chapter 10 Shamanic Journey

Julian, Zelda, Zane and Zanthe patrolled the area around the house to ensure those inside would be safe from harm. They were close to the woods where the pack patrolled who would call the werewolves if the wolves noticed anything or anyone that shouldn't be there.

Willow lit incense, candles and cinnamon in the living room of the house she shared with Waldo. He set out pillows in a circle. The candles, incense and cinnamon were in the center of the circle. Zeta sighed and picked a pillow to sit on. Willow and Waldo sat down too.

Willow looked at Zeta. "You mentioned you haven't been on a shamanic journey before."

Zeta shook her head. "No. I have no idea of what to expect."

Willow smiled. "That's actually good. Just relax and sit comfortably. Take some deep breaths and we'll begin shortly."

Zeta took longer than Willow and Waldo to find a comfortable position. Then she focused on her breathing. Things were quiet and peaceful. The incense and cinnamon was a good combination of smells. The effect made Zeta smile.

Willow said, "Very good. Just keep breathing, Zeta. Go ahead and close your eyes. I'm going to turn on some ambient music to help us get into a trancelike state." She did so.

Zeta blinked. "I like that. It's very relaxing. I see there's a bucket within my reach. You wanted to be prepared in case I get sick."

Willow smiled. "Yeah, I thought it would help just in case you need to throw up."

Zeta smiled. "I appreciate it."

Waldo said, "Okay, let's keep breathing and just let the trance happen. Willow will guide us to the bank and inside the vault." He took a deep breath and closed his eyes.

Zeta reached out and moved the bucket closer to herself. She took more deep breaths and got comfortable. She closed her eyes and waited. Soon she was able to see colors that were calming. She feared nothing in that moment.

Willow's face seemed distant and friendly. It was comforting. Zeta followed every word and found herself walking with Willow and Waldo out in the woods. The moonlight streamed through the trees. Zeta blinked and could see the pack patrolling the area.

She wasn't sure if they could see her and the others walking so close and yet giving the wolves the space they needed to do their job. The trio continued walking until they got close to the bank. They stopped briefly and stared at the ordinary building that glowed in the moonlight in a way that none of the other buildings did in the area.

Willow said, "Now that we can see the bank clearly, something looks off about it."

Zeta said, "None of the other buildings are glowing. The glow looks eerie."

Waldo said, "It does look eerie. I see the ghosts are waiting just over there."

Zeta said, "I can see them now. I understand why they are keeping their distance."

Willow said, "Come on. We need to get inside and get to the vault."

They resumed their walk and just walked through the front door. It was quiet. Zeta could hear some fainting talking. She could feel the dread coming from the trapped souls. They continued to walk across the bank past all the offices and teller windows to the other side where the vault was.

They stopped and stared at it. Something looked off. They stared at the vault door wondering what to do next.

Waldo asked, "Is it open or closed?"

Zeta blinked. "I see the cameras Nebula installed. So, that means we will be seen."

Willow blinked. "This might be a trap. I sense the monster is here."

Zeta said, "He is here. Can't you hear him breathing?"

Waldo turned around. "He's behind us. What should we do now?"

Willow turned around to face the monster. "Oh, he's just human."

The human monster bared his fangs, which were shorter than vampire fangs. "Who are you and what are you doing in my bank?"

Zeta asked, "Are you the CEO?"

"Yes. I have control over all the souls and ghosts here in this bank." He reached out for the trio and then jumped back. "Cinnamon!"

Willow grabbed Waldo and Zeta. "Into the vault now. We must learn more."

They stepped through the vault and studied everything. The CEO monster followed them as closely as he could.

"You won't get away with this! I'll have your souls in the end! I know how to eat them too!" He laughed.

Willow, Waldo and Zeta examined the walls and doors inside the vault. They were soon greeted by those trapped inside.

"What are you doing here?"

"You three don't belong here."

"You need to get out."

"The monster is here!"

Several ghosts screamed.

Willow raised her hands and pure white light shot out of them. The light surrounded all the ghosts, her two companions and herself. The monster was blinded and couldn't follow anyone anymore.

He screamed. "I can't see! How dare you blind me!"

Zeta made mental notes. "Can we get them out of here now?"

Waldo answered, "How do we free them?"

A ghost stepped forward. "I might be able to get out, but the rest are under contract. They are trapped."

Willow sighed. "Those damn contracts again. If we dissolve those, will they be free?"

The ghost answered, "Yes. Now let's get out of here before that monster regains his sight."

Willow led them out of the vault. She kept walking out of the bank and back to the woods. Waldo, Zeta, the ghost stopped once inside of the woods. The other ghosts joined them.

Frankie said, "What did you learn?"

Zeta answered, "Well, the ghost who voluntarily went inside was able to come out with us. The others are still trapped because of their contracts."

Frankie sighed. "Were the missing ghosts inside the bank?"

The once trapped ghost answered, "Yes, they're all there. I hope you living have a way of destroying those contracts."

Zeta blinked. "We'll find away. I just don't know how it will work."

Willow blinked. "I think we can get back to our physical bodies now. We need to let the werewolves and detectives know what we've learned."

The wolves howled. Zeta jumped.

Waldo said, "We need to break the trance. We need to wake

up."

Zeta blinked. "It's the CEO monster coming for us."

Frankie said, "You three go. We'll distract him."

Two large wolves ran into the woods and howled at the monster. Zeta ran. She wasn't sure how to get back to her body and so she just ran back to the house and into the room. She jumped and opened her eyes.

She focused on her breathing. She looked around her and waited.

Waldo opened his eyes. "Are you alright, Zeta?"

"I guess so. Where's Willow?"

Willow opened her eyes. "I'm here."

Waldo put out the incense and the candles. Willow grabbed some cinnamon and put it on Zeta. Then Willow put some on Waldo and herself.

Zeta smelled the cinnamon. "I don't get it. What's wrong with cinnamon?"

Willow answered, "Nothing at all. That soul eating monster can't stand it."

Waldo lit a sage smudge stick and purified the room and the whole house. He stepped outside and smudged the outside of the house and the garden.

Willow studied Zeta's face. "Are you okay? Do you feel sick?"

Zeta took some deep breaths. "No. It's weird. I never felt like throwing up." She blinked. "Is there something wrong with me?"

Willow shrugged. "Perhaps you knew without any doubt where the dread was coming from."

Zeta sighed. "I could hear them talking and I saw all of them."

Willow said, "You were in your light body without your physical body. That probably made the difference."

Zeta said, "We do need to tell the detectives and werewolves what we've learned."

Willow said, "We will. Right now, they are in the woods."

Zeta sighed. "I don't know why I feel so impatient now."

"Perhaps you just want to help the trapped souls?"

"That must be it."

Julian and Zelda ran back to the house and inside. They stopped when they found Zeta and Willow by themselves. Waldo walked into the room a moment later.

Julian asked, "Zeta, are you alright?"

Zeta nodded. "Did you catch him?"

Zelda answered, "I shot him. Zane and Zanthe have him in custody."

Julian sat down next to Zeta. "How was the journey?"

Zeta blinked. "It was strange. The bank glowed in an eerie way and I could see all the trapped souls and the ghosts. I can hear them talking too. It was so vivid."

Willow added, "She didn't get sick this time even though there was a lot of dread.

Zeta nodded. "That was the weird part. They gave me a bucket in case I had to throw up."

Julian smiled. "That was kind. I hope you learned something."

Willow smiled. "We did. One ghost was able to leave the vault with us. They didn't have a contract with the bank. The rest are trapped because of their contracts with the bank."

Zeta said, "So, we need to find a way to destroy those contracts to set them all free."

Zelda said, "I'm letting Zane and Zanthe know. They did find evidence that the bank isn't legal and could be doing money laundering."

Zeta said, "Does that mean there is a way to dissolve those contracts?"

Zelda answered, "There should be a way. I doubt the law would let this bank get away with what it's been doing to its customers. There are laws to protect people from things like overdrafts and automatic loans."

Willow sighed. "That will be a relief to those trapped in the vault."

Zanthe walked into the room. Zane stood right behind her.

"We caught the CEO and he's in a holding cell now. Zelda, we just got your message." She smiled. "Good work finding out how we can set the trapped souls free."

Zane added, "We just need to look into the contracts and see how they compare to the actual laws here in Tigerwood."

Zeta said, "Sounds as if we need to have another firepit meeting."

Willow smiled. "Waldo and I can come if you need us."

Julian said, "Do come. You've done a lot on this case as it is."

Zelda said, "We do need your insight on souls and ghosts. Otherwise, we'd be lost."

Zane said, "I'm glad for everyone's help."

Zanthe said, "Will dissolving the contracts be enough? I thought that trapped ghost without a contract couldn't escape by themself."

Willow blinked. "No, that ghost was able to leave with us. So, we will have to do some magic too."

Zeta said, "That's fine with me."

Waldo smiled. "Good. So, now we know what we need to do next to close this case."

Zane said, "Dissolving the contracts will take time."

Willow blinked. "Zeta mentioned the cameras could see us when we were there."

Zane smiled. "The cameras did pick you up. Let me show you the footage." He pulled out his tablet computer and showed the footage which included them.

Zeta smiled. "Wow, we were glowing as were all the trapped souls."

Zane nodded. "Yes, Nebula did a good job with the cameras."

Zanthe said, "I think they noticed something else when they were installing cameras. It's a big clue to the case."

Zane added, "It ties the bank to the cult without a doubt. The vault seals in souls so they can't escape easily."

Zelda asked, "How long will it take to get through the contracts?"

Zanthe shrugged her shoulders. "I have no idea. I finally got through the part about banks in my education and so it might be easier for me to know what is glaringly wrong with those contracts. The automatic loans is a big part of the problem."

Zane said, "We need to prove the bank was taking advantage of its customers. Then we can shut them down quickly."

Julian asked, "How long can you keep the CEO locked up?"

Zanthe said, "Not long unless we find more connections between him, Cipher and Daren. The cult itself hasn't done anything wrong. Just this person and no one else so far."

Zelda said, "Unless they are aware of what the bank is doing."

Zane said, "That might be hard to prove, but we at least have all the contracts and all the business documents the bank uses."

Zanthe added, "That includes their official and unofficial documents. The official ones are the decoys that they gave to the detectives."

Zelda said, "I figured as much."

Julian said, "The CEO claimed the part about using souls as collateral was just a gimmick and they offer financial literacy classes."

    Zanthe smiled. "There's no proof of those classes. They certainly don't happen in the bank."

Chapter 11 Plan

Once again, everyone assembled around the firepit. Zelda and Jaema held hands. Julian and Zeta held hands. Willow and Waldo held hands. Zane and Zanthe held hands. They were thoughtful and concerned about the people of Tigerwood.

It was the next morning and they were finalizing their plan against the bank. There was no fire in the firepit.

Jaema asked, "So, what's the plan now?"

Zelda answered, "We're pursuing legal means to shut the bank down for their illegal activities. Then we will have to go to the bank to set the trapped souls free."

Jaema said, "Sounds simple, but I know it can't be."

Zanthe said, "Zane and I have discovered a few laws the bank is violating and we can prove money laundering. Now, we just need to get the bank and its CEO for everything they are doing to their customers."

Zeta said, "Willow, Waldo and I will go the bank once the contracts are dissolved and destroyed to set the trapped souls free. It's doubtful anyone will come back to life now, but at least they will be free."

Zane said, "And the ghosts who are currently staying here in Tigerwood will help them to adjust to their new form of existence."

Julian said, "I know I'm nervous about the legal avenue. Do

you really think we can pursue it and win?"

Zanthe nodded. "They are blatantly defying the law and they are acting as if they don't care. Or else the CEO thinks they can continue on with two sets of documents. He wasn't cooperative this morning when we questioned him."

Zane said, "No, he kept denying there are two sets of documents. He doesn't know how we obtained the real ones."

Zelda asked, "Will Nebula have to appear in court today?"

Zanthe shook her head. "No, we are leaving them out of this. Nebula prefers to stay in the background and we're not sure they can maintain any shape long enough for all the questions they would need to answer."

Julian said, "I suppose they aren't necessary for the court case, but they were quite helpful in obtaining the real records and the footage we need."

Zane nodded. "Nebula is proud of it too. They mentioned learning how to appear ghostlike after seeing footage of the ghosts."

Zanthe smiled. "Ariana enjoyed the show."

Everyone laughed.

Zelda asked, "Zanthe, how much longer for your education?"

Zanthe blinked. "I'm almost done. I have some finals to take and hopefully, I will have my degree not too long after that."

Zeta said, "So, then you and Zane can get married."

Zane smiled. "I think it will be better to finish this case before we have our wedding."

Jaema asked, "Is there one more major case to do?"

Zanthe answered, "Yes, just one more. So far the family we've been watching is fine, but that could change once the bank is shut down."

Zelda said, "A bank with a connection to the cult. It's the leader who is a financial backer of the bank?"

Zanthe nodded. "Yes, Daemon is a backer. We haven't found any evidence he's doing anything illegal and we can't find evidence he is aware of what the bank and the CEO are doing."

Zane said, "But we are still watching him."

Zeta sighed. "I'm a bit nervous about what we need to do to free the trapped souls."

Julian squeezed her hand. "I'm sure you'll be fine. You didn't get sick during the shamanic journey."

Zane blinked. "It's interesting she didn't get sick. You usually do whenever you feel dread and fear from others."

Zeta said, "I know. I don't know what was different. Willow thought perhaps because I knew where it was coming from. During the journeying, I could see and hear them too. But I could see and the penguins and the wolves. I don't get it."

Zanthe asked, "Is something changing for Zeta? Perhaps she is learning how to use her gift easier? Or could something physically have changed for her?"

Zane raised an eyebrow. "I have no idea. It is possible she

understands her gift better. She could be different physically too. It's hard to say and I'm not the real expert. Willow knows more about it than I do."

Zelda pulled out her tablet computer and scanned Zeta. She gasped. "Zeta, you're pregnant."

Zeta blinked. "What?" She paused. "We've been using birth control."

Julian gasped. He tried to speak, but nothing came out.

Jaema's eyes widened. "Zeta, are you okay with having a baby?"

Zeta answered, "I don't know. I haven't really thought about it."

Julian said, "Zeta, I'll do what I can to raise the baby with you, if that's what you want." He breathed hard.

Zeta smiled at him. "That's wonderful, Jul. Let's just finish this case first and then we'll do something about the baby."

Zelda sighed. "I knew Jul would take responsibility."

Zane said, "I'll support whatever decision you want."

Zeta's smiled grew. "Your moral support means a lot to me. I didn't expect this and wasn't sure about having any kids." She blinked. "Willow, did you know about the baby?"

Willow smiled. "No. I wasn't paying attention to that part. I didn't even think about it being a possibility."

Waldo smiled. "Well, I give my support too with whatever you decide."

The meeting broke up after that. Willow and Waldo went home to catch up on orders and other things. Jaema and Zeta stayed home to do their work. Jaema monitored the communications and Zeta wrote up notes for the case.

Zane, Zanthe, Zelda and Julian went to the courthouse with the documents they had from the bank. They found where they needed to sit as they waited for the CEO to be brought in. He was escorted in and the judge entered.

Court was in session. No one from the general public was let inside.

The judge looked over the case. "Alright, we have the documents the bank sent us at our request. Nothing looks amiss from them. And then I see two different sets of documents from the police department and from Xenocryst Agency. I also see footage provided from the Guardians." She paused to look over her notes. "Something is very wrong with having two sets of documents. One you send to anyone official asking for them and another set which shows a completely different bank that you keep to yourselves."

The CEO frowned. The judge studied his nonverbal body language.

"I don't see any remorse."

The CEO said, "The Guardians make up all sorts of things. We are a legitimate bank which offers financial literacy classes to our customers so they don't rack up unnecessary debt."

The judge asked, "Where are those classes held?"

"In my bank of course."

The judge frowned. "I've seen the footage from your own security cameras and the ones the Guardians installed. There are no classes at your bank. Those times you are referring to are when you get people to sign the contracts which use their souls for collateral."

The CEO gasped. "What?"

The judge continued, "Furthermore, the footage does show ghosts trapped in the bank vault instead of money. From a legal standpoint, souls cannot be used as collateral for loans because collateral needs to be something physical. Souls are not physical. So, that's a strike against you and your bank."

She paused to read her notes. "Next we have your clause which states no overdraft protections. Instead you give them loans which are short termed. When people can't make payments, you take their souls. I've seen the footage on that and it's truly creepy. Then your employees dump the bodies in the woods. You didn't renegotiate with your customers. The contracts are all in your favor."

She glared at the CEO. "Then there is the matter of where you get your money. We know you have connections with criminals and that the bank is a way to launder the money to make it look legal. I see you've made deals with Cipher and Daren. Cipher may be dead, but Daren is not. He's in prison and he will not get out now."

The CEO gaped.

The judge asked, "Zanthe, do you or Xenocryst Agency or the Guardians have anything to add?"

Zanthe looked at everyone and then back at the judge. "No, your Honor. That's all we had to bring to your attention."

The judge said, "Then so be it. I now will make my judgement. I will issue an order shut down the bank and dissolve all contracts with its customers to be enacted immediately. As for the CEO, he will go to prison." She hit her gravel. Then stood up to leave the courtroom.

The CEO was taken away to be processed and sent to prison. The detectives and the werewolves sighed at different times. They stood up and left the courthouse. They knew there was one thing left to do and that they would be there to ensure the bank was shut down and the trapped souls were free.

For now, Zane and Zanthe went back to the police station to check on things there. Zelda and Julian went home to tell their wives the news. They then made arrangements with Willow and Waldo when they would all go to the bank.

While Zanthe waited for the order to shut down the bank to go into effect, she took her finals. Zane checked on the police at the station and left her alone. It was the calm before the storm and no one knew what to expect.

Zanthe smiled once she was done with her test. She didn't

worry as she had done all she could do to get her degree. Now, she was ready to finish the case. Her test results arrived before the order to shut down the bank. She ran out of the office.

"Zane!"

He turned around. "What is it?"

"I got my degree!"

He smiled and hugged her. The police cheered. Then the order arrived and everyone got right back to work. The detectives were called. Zeta went to Willow and Waldo's place to get ready with them.

All in all, things were moving fast now.

Chapter 12 Magic

Willow, Waldo and Zeta walked down the street. They were determined in their mission. Zeta had learned how to put up a shield and hoped it would last. The closer they all got to the bank, the more the dread was beginning to rise.

Zelda, Julian, Zane and Zanthe arrived at the bank first with the order to shut down the bank. Zanthe showed the order to the greeter.

The greeter frowned. "Did you arrest my boss?"

Zanthe nodded. "Yes, we did. This bank is illegal and has to be shut down immediately per court order."

The greeter's frown deepened. "What about the rest of us who work here?"

Zanthe answered, "The social workers will be arriving shortly to help you all transition to new jobs without losing your homes."

The greeter blinked. "What?"

Zanthe smiled as social workers entered the bank. They approached the tellers first.

She gestured to the newcomers. "As you can see, they are starting with the most vulnerable. In this case, it's the tellers who might find it hard to get jobs next after what the CEO has done."

The greeter scoffed. "That's not helping me."

Zanthe raised an eyebrow. "They will get to you. In the meantime, we are dissolving the contracts and setting the trapped souls free."

The greeter sneered. "Very well, but I think you will find it will be impossible to set the souls free."

Zanthe asked, "Why is that?"

"Souls aren't real as everyone knows."

Zanthe smiled. "Some of my colleagues have already set free a ghost who got trapped inside your bank. So, I don't doubt they will set the rest of them free without any trouble."

The greeter sighed. "You have an answer for everything. Fine." She blinked and read the order. She again sighed. "Very well, the contracts are dissolved. We are in the process of giving back all the money to our customers who are still alive." She activated the computer terminal and dissolved the contracts and sent out messages to current customers. She looked back to Zanthe. "I hope you're happy now. Not only am I unemployed now, but I have pulled the plug on this whole bank. Daemon won't be happy about this."

Zanthe raised an eyebrow. "Do you know him personally?"

"Yes. I know him quite well. You may go into the vault." The greeter unlocked the vault. "Do what you need to do. I'm done with this business." She paused to watch the social workers helping the tellers. "Are you sure they won't forget me?"

Zanthe answered, "They won't. If you're done, you can walk

over to them now to get started."

The greeter sighed wither her frozen botox face and walked over to the social workers. Zanthe turned to look at everyone who came with her.

Willow said, "We're ready."

Zanthe said, "The vault should be unlocked. I'm sure we all heard it unlock. Be careful."

Willow nodded. "Anything else we need to know about?"

Zane answered, "I'm checking the computer now. Nebula mentioned there might be a few things to deactivate before going into the vault." He used the computer. "Ah, I see a few things. This will take some time."

Zeta said, "That's fine with me."

Zelda asked, "So, is this it for the bank?"

Zanthe blinked. "I think so. Zane, are you seeing the contracts dissolved?"

Zane answered, "Yes, they are all dissolved and notification have been sent out as she said. I don't know if she was aware of all the security for the vault. And for the bank too. Some of these are a little weird, but I can see how they would trap ghosts or souls inside."

Willow stepped over to the screen. "That is weird. Can you deactivate all of that?"

Zane answered, "Most of it. However, I do recall a ghost was able to leave with you. Do you know how that was possible beyond they didn't have a contract with the bank?"

Willow blinked. "The ghost piggy backed off of us. So, we may have to let the trapped souls do the same."

Zane blinked. His tablet beeped. He pulled it out and checked it. "The ghosts are gathering outside. They are standing by for the trapped souls."

Willow smiled. "So, we are making progress. I'm sure the other ghosts will be able to help out too."

Zane said, "I don't doubt that for a minute." He saw a message. "Nebula knows what I'm doing and is giving some suggestions on how to deactivate all the security in the vault and around the building itself."

Willow's smile got bigger. "That's great." She turned to Waldo and Zeta. "Are you two ready to go into the vault?"

Waldo nodded.

Zeta bit her lip. "I suppose so."

Julian squeezed her hand. "I'm sure it will be fine."

Willow said, "I can purify you afterwards, especially with the baby."

Zeta nodded. "That will help out."

Zelda looked around. "Zanthe, do you want us to do some exit interviews with the former employees before they leave?"

Zanthe answered, "That's not a bad idea."

Julian squeezed his wife's hand again. "Good luck. I'm going with Zelda for the exit interviews."

Zeta squeezed his hand. "I need to help set some souls free."

They let go of each other's hands. He left with Zelda to interview some employees. Zeta waited for Zane and Nebula to finish deactivating the security. It took more time. Zeta blinked and watched the detectives do their interviews. She could see employees leave one or two at time from the building.

The social workers finished and left the building with the rest of the employees. Then Zeta felt them all around her. They were hopeful. She couldn't see them, but she knew it was the ghosts who wanted to help set the souls free from the bank and help them adjust to life as ghosts.

She smiled and turned back to Zane.

He smiled. "Alright, everything is deactivated. I'm sure you three know what to do next."

Willow nodded. She walked to the other side of the building with Waldo and Zeta in tow. Willow opened the door to the vault and could see the trapped souls inside puzzled as to what was going on.

She smiled at them. "Everyone, we have good news for you. Your contracts have been dissolved and the security in the vault and around the bank has been deactivated. You're free to go."

The souls gasped. "What? Just like that?"

Willow nodded. "If you're finding it's still too hard, we have other ghosts here who want to help you adjust to your new life. You can also piggy back off of us and we can walk out of the bank together."

The souls hesitated. They weren't sure what to do.

Frankie walked past Willow. "Hello, new people. I'm Frankie. I'm here to help you transition. I'm sure many of you are confused and scared, but there are many of us that live as ghosts. Just keep in mind the living may not be aware of us. Don't take it personally."

"Uh, Frankie, do we need to worry about our debts?"

Frankie shook her head. "We don't have money in the spirit realm. However, there are other things we can work on that we couldn't while we were alive. We know you were taken advantage of and that it can be a shock to know your physical bodies are dead, but you still feel alive in some ways."

Many of the souls agreed with that last statement.

"So, we should just leave with you and we'll be alright?"

Frankie nodded. "Yes, just come with us. Willow, Waldo and Zeta are good anchors to help you out of the building. Then please let go of them. We can help you from there. This building isn't safe for us to stay here much longer."

The souls cheered. They finally felt overwhelming hope for their futures.

Willow said, "Alright, let's walk out of the bank. This way, everyone."

Waldo and Zeta smiled and followed Willow out of the bank. Zane and Zanthe waited until they had reached the door before following the whole procession. The werewolves were the last ones out of the building and they waited until they knew all the ghosts and souls were outside. Zelda and Julian had finished their interviews and waited for everyone to come out.

Zane closed the door behind everyone. He scanned the area. "Alright, good. Everyone got out safely. No one, living or ghost, are still inside." He let the security system to turn itself back on. "The security system is turning itself back on, so no one try to get back inside."

Frankie said, "We don't want to go back. Let's go everyone. We have new people to acclimate." The ghosts disappeared.

Willow said, "For those who couldn't see or hear the ghosts, they have left the area."

Zeta smiled. "They are feeling more hopeful than when they were trapped."

Zanthe said, "I'm sure it will still be an adjustment, but they will be fine with Frankie leading the way."

Julian said, "Is there anything else we need to do now?"

Zane looked over notes on his tablet. "I don't see much of anything."

Zanthe answered, "We do need to file with the court that we shut the bank down and what the employees said."

Zelda said, "Then let's do that now and get it over with."

Willow asked, "Do you need Waldo or me for that?"

Zanthe answered, "No, your part is done."

Zeta said, "Do you need me for anything?"

Zanthe smiled. "I think you can go too. It shouldn't take us too long to finish up."

Zeta said, "Then meet us at the firepit tonight. I need to ensure I have all my notes for the book."

Zanthe chuckled. "Of course we'll be there."

The werewolves and the detectives went to the court to finish up the paperwork. Willow, Waldo and Zeta went to witches' place. They were quiet during their walk. When they had finally arrived at the place, there were lots of ghosts there to greet them.

Willow laughed. "So, they decided to come here!"

Waldo smiled. "I suppose they could stay for a while. It's not as if we have to look after them."

Zeta laughed. "It's your house. I think the wolves and other animals are okay with the ghosts in the woods."

Frankie said, "You bet the animals don't mind us. We figured we'd hang out here to give the new ghosts a safe place to hang out. We thought your place was good as it's safe and we'll do our best to stay out of your way. Some might even like to help with your magic."

Willow said, "That's fine with me. We were just going to purify ourselves especially now that Zeta has to decide about the little one inside of her."

The ghosts cheered.

Zeta said, "I'm not sure I can kill her. I think my husband and I need to plan how to take care of her."

Willow smiled. "That's one way to deal with it."

Waldo lit some incense and a smudge stick. He waved it around Willow, Zeta and himself and offered some to the ghosts.

The ghosts were grateful for the support. Some weren't sure how long it would take them to adjust to being ghosts without physical bodies to deal with.

One ghost asked, "Where is my physical body buried?"

Frankie answered, "Where you requested it to be in writing. If you're unsure of where that is, you can see Eugenia who took care of your physical body for burial."

"She took over for you?"

Frankie nodded. "She did. She's just as good as I was. So, you needn't worry about anything. She just prefers to go over what you put in writing and then get your feedback as she works. For some of you, she didn't get to do that and it bothered her."

"So, we can check what she did and let her know what we think. Would that help her to feel better?"

Frankie smiled. "It would indeed."

Zeta relaxed and smelled the incense. She couldn't see the ghosts, but she felt their nearness and their hopes. She wasn't worried about anything at all. She looked forward to the evening when she could light another fire in the firepit. Then they could discuss the case and how it turned out.

Of course there would be another case and a new baby to welcome into the world. Oh, and a wedding. Zeta beamed knowing the werewolves were still planning it and wondered what they wanted for the ceremony and the reception.

Chapter 13 Werewolf Wedding

Zeta lit the fire in the firepit as everyone sat down. Zelda and Jaema sat next to each other. Julian sat down and waited for Zeta to sit next to him. She did so just as Zane and Zanthe found their seats. Then Willow and Waldo sat down.

Jaema said, "I'm glad this case is over. It was giving me the creeps."

Zeta said, "I think lots of other people felt the same way."

Julian said, "But there's still one more case."

Zelda asked, "What about the cult that Daemon leads? Will he be arrested for the bank venture?"

Zanthe sighed. "We don't have anything against him or the cult. We know the CEO was a part of the cult, but we can't prove that Daemon knew the bank was using souls as collateral. He was just an investor and we can't prove he knows anything more about it."

Zelda sighed. "I see. What about Eugenia's relatives?"

Zanthe answered, "They're fine for now. Nothing out of the ordinary has happened to them."

Zane said, "The police are still surveying them just to be safe. As far as we know something could happen to the family according to the data left behind by both Cipher and Daren."

Julian sighed. "I hate waiting for something bad to happen to them."

Zanthe said, "I do too, but we can't do anything until something does."

Zane blinked. "Or if something suspicious happens."

Zelda asked, "Is that likely from the family itself?"

Zanthe blinked. "From what the police have told me who are watching them, the family seems fairly ordinary."

Willow sighed. "I've had a few run ins with Daemon and his cult. They weren't pleasant. I've used defensive magic against them. So far they've been leaving me alone."

Zeta asked, "Did they want you to talk to the dead?"

Willow nodded. "They heard of my gifts and thought I'd do whatever they wanted. They were forceful and mean about it."

Zeta sighed. "So, coercion. Perhaps they want the young girl because the young are thought to be more malleable than adults."

Zelda raised an eyebrow. "That could be. Or perhaps they think she's too young and inexperienced to understand how to use her gifts and talents and they can step in and train her. Then they can use her for her gifts and talents."

Willow blinked. "That's probably why they are interested in her. I refused and fought back when they came for me. Have they tried to go after Eugenia?"

Zanthe answered, "I don't think so. She wasn't aware of the cult when I asked her about it."

Zeta said, "Perhaps Frankie and the other ghosts protect her."

Willow smiled. "That wouldn't be surprising. I know how fond Frankie was of Eugenia when the older woman was still alive."

Zanthe said, "I hope the young girl has some protection too."

Zane said, "I'm sure we'll find out soon enough if she doesn't."

Jaema asked, "Zeta, are you ready to write the book for this case?"

Zeta nodded. "I have all the notes for it and the outline is done. I'll start drafting tomorrow."

Zane asked, "Are you still coming to our wedding?"

Zeta smiled. "Of course. I mean when I'm not at your wedding."

Everyone laughed.

Zeta and Jaema helped Zanthe get ready as Julian and Zelda helped Zane get ready in another room. The werewolves were nervous. The bride and groom were separated for now. Willow and Waldo arrived and waited for everyone to assemble outside of the werewolves' home.

Zanthe bit her lip. "Did you two feel this way when you were getting ready?"

Jaema smiled. "Well, we were able to get ready with Alara and I think that helped. Three nervous brides who could help each other and laugh with each other."

Zeta smiled. "That was fun. She and Oliver are doing well

on their show. They are considering having kids."

Zanthe smiled. "We haven't decided yet. Zane is so considerate about the whole thing. I think we just need to get used to being married first."

Zeta said, "That's a good idea."

Zanthe asked, "Zeta, have you decided?"

Zeta said, "I told Julian as long as the baby and I are okay, that we might as well go through with it."

Jaema added, "We're all getting excited and trying to figure out where and how we will keep the baby safe."

Zeta said, "We may have to build another tiny house just for the kid."

Zanthe laughed.

Julian said, "We can hear."

Zeta said, "Good. Jul, we're going to keep the baby with us in our house until she is old enough to start looking after herself. Then she will have to have a little house of her own."

Julian laughed. "Whatever you say, dear."

Zelda said, "Jaema, are you thinking about having a baby now?"

Jaema laughed. "No. I'm thinking about being aunt to their baby."

Zelda laughed. "I wouldn't mind being aunt."

Zane said, "I'm in no rush, Zanthe."

Zanthe laughed. "Good. Okay, I think you two have fussed

over me enough. Are you ready, Zane?"

"As ready as I'm going to be."

Everyone stepped out to meet Willow and Waldo.

Willow looked at everyone. "Is everyone ready to start?"

Zane and Zanthe took each other's hands and stood in front of Willow.

Willow smiled. "We gather here today to celebrate the union between Zanthe and Zane. Does anyone here object to what this marriage?"

No one said anything. A cloud floated near them with Ariana smiling on top of it. The cloud landed and she stepped off.

"Zanthe, we couldn't miss your wedding."

The cloud formed into a humanoid who couldn't maintain their shape very long. "Hello, everyone."

Willow blinked. "So, I take it there are no objections to this marriage."

Everyone shouted, "Yay for Zanthe and Zane!" They laughed.

Willow continued to smile. "Then let's hear the couple's vows."

The couple looked into each other's eyes and exchanged their vows. Then they slipped rings on each other's fingers and kissed. Everyone cheered again and clapped.

Willow smiled. "Alright, you are now married. It's time to dance and celebrate your union."

Waldo turned on some music. Zane bowed to Zanthe and she

bowed back. They reached out for each other and danced in front of everyone. There was more cheering while they danced their first dance as an official couple.

When the song ended, another one began and everyone else joined in the couple dancing. They had fun and continued to dance long after the sun went down.

From the edge of the woods, Daemon and Dario stood by and watched the wedding. Daemon frowned at the couples.

Dario said, "So, they shut the bank down. What are we going to do now?"

Daemon's frown deepened. "We will have to get the girl then. We will need her. Our best ghost talker is in prison with Daren."

Dario said, "Then we need to take out her parents. Then we will have her."

Daemon raised an eyebrow. "We could do that. I believe we have an assassin in our group. What else? Does she have any other family?"

Dario blinked. "No one that's important."

"I thought she was related to the undertaker Eugenia."

Dario continued, "She is related to Eugenia, but you know we've tried to get to her. Do you remember what happened?"

"Frankie got to her first. Damn that woman."

"She's dead now."

"Yet, we still can't get to Eugenia. What is with the funeral home she inherited from Frankie?"

Dario sighed. "I don't get it. I tried talking to Eugenia once when she was in between jobs. She blew me off."

Daemon said, "She sounds as bad as Willow."

Dario said, "They're too powerful and too independent."

"That's why we need the girl. She couldn't be that independent. She probably doesn't know how to use her powers yet."

Dario said, "That's what I'm thinking. We need to isolate her from her parents and then we can influence her."

Daemon smiled. "That would be great if we could do that. We need a powerful ghost whisperer. The rest are either dead or in prison. It's all the fault of those people over there. They can celebrate now, but we will get them sooner or later."

Dario said, "Of course we will. They can't be that great."

Daemon said, "They stopped all the prior plans. It's too bad we lost the police captain. With him, we would be able to turn Tigerwood into what we wanted. Now there is a new police captain and she's a werewolf defending the people."

Dario said, "And she's now married to a werewolf too. It would be awful if they had any kids."

The moon rose and shone in the sky. The wolves saw the two people standing around. They barked and howled at the strangers.

Dario jumped. "What is this?"

Daemon scowled. "That's the pack who patrols the woods

now. We need to go before they get the attention of the police."

The wolves continued to howl. The wedding party broke up. The werewolves walked over to the woods. Dario ran off. Daemon pulled his hood of his cloak over his head to hide his face. He ran off in a different direction.

Zane and Zanthe looked around. The wolves got quiet.

"Zane, whoever it was ran off. They're gone."

He sighed. "This can't be a good sign."

"Probably not. The wolves say they were up to no good and they were watching us."

Zane raised an eyebrow. "Could that have been Daemon?"

Zanthe shrugged. "Hard to say. The pack doesn't know who he is. They don't know his smell."

"Not yet, but I wouldn't be surprised if they will learn or they already have and didn't realize it was he."

"Now what are we going to do?"

"Do? We can't do anything about them yet. We know it's a matter of time before the cult goes after the young girl. In the meantime, we can have our wedding night."

She blinked. "I suppose that's the best thing to do. Everyone said their goodbyes and they are leaving now. Will we have time for a honeymoon?"

"I don't know, but we do deserve some downtime after everything we've done."

"Alright, let's go home and enjoy ourselves." She took his hand.

They said goodbye to the wolves and walked back to their house. They stepped inside and locked the door. The guests had already left and were well on their way to their homes. The werewolves weren't entirely sure what to do and didn't worry about it.

They helped each other undress and experimented and learned what each other liked. No one bothered them and they could enjoy themselves and get used to being married.

The detectives and their wives went home to plan on how they would handle having a baby on the property. They focused on every little detail and came up with different plans on how to handle if something would go wrong with the pregnancy or delivery.

They didn't care how long it took to plan. They were too excited to worry about anything else. They didn't worry that the pack had found two suspicious characters at the edge of the woods. They knew the werewolves would take care of it.

For now, the talk centered on the new baby and what they would do to take care of her and how they would do their best to not let her ruin their detective agency they had all worked hard to build.

The baby had no idea of such things. She couldn't even dream of wrecking anyone's life. She dreamed of being cared for in a safe place surrounded by love.

Also By Ali Noel Vyain

For more information, please visit

alinoelvyain.wordpress.com

and books2read.com/alinoelvyain

The Strange & Unusual Universe of Silver Moon Unicorn

The Colonies of Earth Series
The Colonies of Earth (Eris): Different
The Colonies of Earth (Venus): In Men's Shadows
The Colonies of Earth Series: Tales From Mars
The Colonies of Earth: The Colonies Will Be Independent
The Colonies of Earth: (Orcus): The Amazons Rise Up
The Colonies of Earth (Pluto): First Time
The Colonies of Earth (Saturn & Titan): Praying for Death
The Colonies of Earth (Mercury): This Strange, Wild Land
The Colonies of Earth (The Moon): The Crossroads
The Colonies of Earth (Triton): The Mistress
The Colonies of Earth (Neptune): The Plantation Owner
The Colonies of Earth (Ceres): The Vampire's Girlfriend
The Colonies of Earth (Titania): Vampire Struggles
The Colonies of Earth (Haumea): Aftermath
The Colonies of Earth: Box Set

The Starlover Series
Book 1: Project Earth
Book 2: Uncle & Niece
Book 3: Traveling Teenager
Book 4: Cassandra the Red Tiger
The Starlover Series Box Set

The Violet Series
Book 1: A Water Nymph's Tale
Book 2: The Search for Merlin
Book 3: Retribution
Book 4: Flames & Ghosts
Book 5: The Lunatics
Book 6: Witches & Weres
Book 7: Recovery
Book 8: To Love or Not to Love
Book 9: The Joys of Working with Others
Book 10: After the Affair is Over
Book 11: No More Quarantine
Book 12: The Amazons Are Still in Control
Book 13: Family History
The Violet Series Box Set

The Guardian Series
Book 1: Formation of the Guardians

Book 2: The Sorceress and the Prince
Book 3: The Escaped Courtier
Book 4: The War Must End
Book 5: Anjilina
Book 6: Maggie the Fairy Warrior
Book 7: Faedin Hides From the World
Book 8: Raelon's Discovery
Book 9: The Dragons of the Four Realms
Book 10: Faedin Returns
Book 11: Paradise Regained
Book 12: Grand Rock Junction
Book 13: Crime of Love
Book 14: The Lost Glory of Elsewhere
The Guardian Series Box Set

The White Lion Unicorn Series
Book 1: A Colony of Tiny Nekos
Book 2: The Cats of Elsewhere
Book 3: Her Name is Elsewhere
Book 4: The Death of Elsewhere
Book 5: The Black Unicorn and the Winged Lion
Book 6: The Rebirth of Elsewhere
Book 7: The Childhood of Elsewhere
Book 8: The Adolescence of Elsewhere
Book 9: Elsewhere City & Spirit

The White Lion Unicorn Series Box Set

The Titanium Mysteries
Book 1: What Is She Doing Here?
Book 2: Werewolves
Book 3: Zombies
Book 4: Vampires
Book 5: For the Children
Book 6: Evil Snowpeople
Book 7: The Mortuary
Book 8: Missed Wedding
Book 9: Virtual Game
Book 10: Charm School Failure
Book 11: The Ultimate Bomb Manual
Book 12: The Bank
Book 13: The Flawless Plan
The Titanium Mysteries Box Set

Cyborgs
Book 1: Who is Augustus Edmunch?
Book 2: Byte Back
Book 3: The Greatest Hackers in the Universe
Cyborgs Box Set

Alice Flowers Tarot

Madeline Austen Tarot Deck
Story 1: The Fool
Story 2: 2 of Swords
Story 3: The Devil
Story 4: 7 of Cups
Story 5: 5 of Pentacles
Story 6: 5 of Wands
Story 7: 5 of Swords
Story 8: 5 of Cups
Story 9: 8 of Swords
Story 10: Wheel of Fortune
Story 11: The Hanged Person
Story 12: 2 of Cups
Story 13: The Magician
Story 14: 4 of Pentacles
Story 15: 6 of Pentacles
Story 16: 10 of Wands
Story 17: 10 of Swords
Story 18: 3 of Swords
Story 19: 9 of Swords
Story 20: 4 of Swords
Story 21: 7 of Swords
Story 22: 2 of Pentacles
Story 23: 2 of Wands
Story 24: 6 of Cups

Story 25: 4 of Cups
Story 26: 7 of Pentacles
Story 27: 3 of Pentacles
Story 28: 8 of Cups
Story 29: Page of Swords
Story 30: Page of Cups
Story 31: Page of Pentacles
Story 32: Page of Wands
Story 33: Knight of Swords
Story 34: Knight of Cups
Story 35: Knight of Pentacles
Story 36: Knight of Wands
Story 37: Queen of Swords
Story 38: Queen of Cups
Story 39: Queen of Pentacles
Story 40: Queen of Wands
Story 41: King of Swords
Story 42: King of Cups
Story 43: King of Pentacles
Story 44: King of Wands
Story 45: 9 of Wands
Story 46: 8 of Wands
Story 47: 3 of Wands
Story 48: 6 of Wands
Story 49: 3 of Cups

Story 50: 9 of Cups
Story 51: 10 of Cups
Story 52: 8 of Pentacles
Story 53: 9 of Pentacles
Story 54: Ace of Swords
Story 55: Ace of Cups
Story 56: Ace of Pentacles
Story 57: Ace of Wands
Story 58: 10 of Pentacles
Story 59: The Chariot
Story 60: The Star
Story 61: The Moon
Story 62: The Hermit
Story 63: The Sun
Story 64: Strength
Story 65: Justice
Story 66: Judgement
Story 67: Temperance
Story 68: The Tower
Story 69: Death
Story 70: 6 of Swords
Story 71: 7 of Wands
Story 72: 4 of Wands
Story 73: The Lovers
Story 74: The Hierophant or High Priest

Story 75: The High Priestess
Story 76: Emperor
Story 77: Empress
Story 78: The World
Alice Flowers Tarot (box set)

Background Informational Books
Planets of the Universe
Dr. Butterfly's Guide to People of the Universe
The City of Elsewhere, Platinum
Modern Mordor

Cat Tale Books
Cat Tales of the Frisky9 Scarf Army
Frisky's Friends and Scarves
Cat Fairy Tales

Sir Socks Le Chat
The Life Adventures of Sir Socks Le Chat
The Diary of Sir Socks Le Chat
The Afterlife Adventures of Sir Socks Le Chat
Sir Socks Le Chat (a box set)

Poetry

Scientist in Training Gone Mad
Honoring the Cats in My Life
Thoughts on Turning 40
Transitions
Unexpected
By Accident of Birth
Failure
Mental Illness
Insanity
In the Name of Survival
Food or Poison
Myths
Becoming a Black Unicorn
All About Cats
Medusa
Night Hags
The Desert
Content Creator
Discounted
Drugs
Falling in Love
The 7 Deadly Sins of Xmas
Fragments
Unrealistic Expectations
Deviation

Changling

Non-Fiction Books
Publishing 101: How to Publish Books While Spending Little to No Money at All
How to Build Ebooks Using XHTML & Calibre
Hyperspace
Various Articles